PRAISE FOR
JACKSON PARK

"In *Jackson Park*, Charlotte Carter blends
street savvy with wry urbanity and delivers
a truly modern big-city crime tale."
—MARGO JEFFERSON

ACCLAIM FOR CHARLOTTE CARTER
AND HER NANETTE HAYES MYSTERIES

COQ AU VIN

"High-spirited . . . Terrific charm . . . Infectious energy."
—MARILYN STASIO, *The New York Times Book Review*

"Absorbing . . . A witty, erotic, and moving love song
to Paris and its 'glamorous black past.' "
—*Detroit Free Press*

"A fun book . . . Nanette is charming . . . .with perfect
taste, and we'll gladly follow her anywhere."
—*Rocky Mountain News*

RHODE ISLAND RED

"Wholly delightful . . . The year's freshest crime debut."
—*GQ*

"Extraordinary . . . Carter has added a refreshingly
new kind of private dick to the market."
—*Paper*

"A dazzler . . . Style and atmosphere are
the keys to this jazz-drenched story."
—*Ellery Queen's Mystery Magazine*

JACKSON PARK

CHARLOTTE CARTER

BALLANTINE BOOKS • NEW YORK

A One World Book
Published by The Random House Ballantine Publishing Group

Copyright © 2003 by Charlotte Carter

All rights reserved under International and Pan-American
Copyright Conventions. Published in the United States
by The Random House Ballantine Publishing Group, a division of
Random House, Inc., New York, and simultaneously in Canada
by Random House of Canada Limited, Toronto.

www.ballantinebooks.com/one/

Library of Congress Cataloging-in-Publication Data
Carter, Charlotte.
Jackson Park / by Charlotte Carter.—1st ed.
p.   cm.
ISBN 0-345-44782-4
I. Title.
PS3603.A776 J33 2002
813'.6—dc21   2002026259

Manufactured in the United States of America

First Edition: August 2003

2 4 6 8 10 9 7 5 3 1

AUTHOR'S NOTE

The various Chicago neighborhoods described in this novel—
the South Side, the Loop, etc.—do exist, but Forest Street is
imaginary. Likewise, the book mingles fictional place names,
such as Champlain Elementary School, with actual ones.

JACKSON PARK

PROLOGUE

If things had gone just a little bit differently—another little turn of the wheel—I might have gone out in a blaze of gunfire. They'd have *taken* me out, like they did the white guy in the Texas tower. Or I might be sending imaginary telegrams from a padded cell. For sure, I wouldn't have fulfilled my dream of going to college.

For the longest while, see, nobody liked me.

Sure, a lot of kids think that. But by the time I was nine I had amassed some pretty powerful evidence. For instance:

1. My mother remarried—or was she marrying for the first time? I've never been totally clear on that—and moved far away. In any case, she forgot to send me the new address.

2. Responsibility for my care fell to my grandmother, who kept me clean and reasonably righteous. But she was essentially a pitiless old bat whose fortitude and patience were all gone by the time we wound up together. Not only did her husband die young, but, one by one, her children had turned into living disappointments, and whatever coddling kindness she may have once owned had long ago been drained off by her hard years of working as a domestic. Not her fault, I know. But not mine, either. I got cheated out of the hot buttered biscuits, the massive loving arms, and the sturdy black lap that the race boosters are always touting.

3. I did get one good break when I was gifted with a love of reading. But even that turned out to have a downside. I became the worst kind of kissass teacher's pet. I was showered with gold stars, spelling medals, and A's—and regular beatings from classmates who hated my goody-goody, library-loving, gimpy left foot ass from day one.

4. Remember Mr. Polio and the swath he cut through America during the 1950s? Well, he came and got my sweet young cousin Dot—my only playmate and confidante. She would have to be the one that bastard took, right? The soft spoken one who liked to braid my hair and never laughed at the way I jumped hopscotch and knew even at age nine how to hold a person close to heart and make her not afraid. Dot's ignorant father had heard somewhere that the Salk vaccine

actually contained the virus, and so he would not allow her to have the shot.

My cousin was just a little kid. And she was dead. That tore it.

With her death, the scorn of my peers and their snowballs and their signifying about my ugly lace-up shoes became a matter of indifference to me. Furthermore, I decided it was high time for some payback. No more taking the long way home in order to avoid the kids at the end of the block who delighted in ripping up my workbooks. Let them push me down; I was impervious. No more crying in my room and achy half memories of my mother throughout the night. My dreams became happy ones where I liquefied enemies with my rage.

My enemies were legion. I wasn't going to stop with school bullies and short-changing shopkeepers, though. No. My thinking was much larger than that—it was global. I hadn't yet figured out what form it would take, but my vengeance was going to be absolutely biblical.

Luckily, Grandma Rosetta died just then. Died a hero, actually: she'd never know it, but she saved the world from the havoc I was about to unleash upon it. For I was taken in and raised by her sister, Ivy. And along with a hundred other miracles that occurred under the loving guidance of my great-aunt and her husband, Woodson, I lost all interest in being a notorious Negro girl sociopath.

ONE

Chicago, 1968

Just how good was the good life for us over there in Africa? It kind of makes you wonder.

Long before there was a South Side of Chicago, I mean. Long before the Afro pick or the Negro spiritual or George Wallace. Before the martyred students at the lunch counters and under the quicklime. Before heroin and tap dancing, before the Harlem Renaissance and before the nightmare of the real *Gone with the Wind*.

To hear the poets tell it, we were all kings and princes. But I don't think I was. I think I was an ordinary Joe—make that Jill, as I am a girl—and I was probably just as fucked up and out of it as I am today.

But what's the use of that kind of speculation? The point is, they came and got us. Royal lineage or no, it was the cotton patch, the missy's kitchen, and the massah's bed.

And so the slave called Solomon Lisle begat the one called Edmond who begat Arthur who begat Harold and Leland—and oh, there was an awful lot of that going on over the course of some two hundred years. Ultimately, in the American belle epoque, my great-uncle Woody was begat.

Most of the Lisle men sired offspring at will. Woody's lovely wife Ivy wanted babies so much, she did everything short of visiting a witch doctor. They tried and tried, but she was unable to have children. Be careful what you wish for, the saying goes. They wound up with me.

Despite that little joke that fate played on them, they nourished and loved me, and now I'm almost twenty. They even pop for most of my tuition at Debs College, where I'm an English major, making me the inadvertent token in that august department.

Debs College looks more like an office building than a university. Situated in the middle of the Loop, its campus is the whole of downtown Chicago, and for a quad we have the splendor of Grant Park, as commodious a place to sit and think as any that I could imagine.

So why in hell am I in the underlit, smoke-laden student hangout bar, whimsically named the Yacht Club, making lists on a paper napkin of the names of Woody's forebears?

I'm half drunk and I'm stalling, that's why. I have to go and see a goodly number of the clan at the annual Lisle family gala, being held tonight at the Parkway Inn. I'm already forty minutes late.

Hard to believe: MLK is eight days dead. And here I am on a barstool trying to recall the names of some distant cousins who live in Joliet. It seems so strange. But then, everything has taken on a kind of unreality since they murdered Dr. King.

My friend Bobby Vaughan came in and took the stool next to mine.

"Hey, Cassandra."

"Hey. I couldn't get a booth," I said. "It's packed in here tonight."

The Yacht Club was in fact crowded every Friday evening. In addition to the usual mix of customers, downtown office workers tended to come in on Friday to celebrate week's end with communal pizzas and too much to drink.

Bobby ordered a beer.

"How come you're here, Vaughan? No hot date on a Friday night? That doesn't sound like you."

"I'm getting together with somebody—later."

"That's more like it. A midnight rendezvous. Have fun."

He laughed indulgently. "Don't get carried away, Cassandra. We going to a movie at seven-thirty. Seven-thirty ain't midnight."

As unlikely as it was, Bobby was my closest friend, emphasis on *friend*. Not that I wasn't happy with that—I was, I loved him—but sometimes I let myself wonder if he'd ever look at me in a different way. I told myself all the time: if you were normal, he might. If you weren't so goddamn odd looking, he might one day look at you the way he looks at the girls he sleeps with.

I should say "the sisters" he sleeps with, shouldn't I? Except I knew more about Bobby Vaughan than he thought I knew. His sex life was not limited to black women, no matter how quiet he kept that.

I had no business wondering about that stuff, though. Bobby was tall and strong and as handsome as the wild chestnut mount in a girl's illustrated story book. He attracted more female attention than he could have handled in three lifetimes.

I never had that kind of problem. Men have a habit of looking right through me. I'm carrying about twenty pounds more than I need. I'm not ugly, exactly, but I have a face devoid of any lovely planes or angles and my red hair, which I wear in a fat braid down my back, is neither kinky nor romantically curly; it is simply unruly. Nearsighted, I wear rimless spectacles, which, thanks partly to John Lennon, have become fashionable. I remember looking over at another student one day during chemistry class. He was drawing caricatures of various people in the room, including the professor, an almost freakishly tall young white man the students had nicknamed Bird Boy. I was featured on the sketch pad as well, as a barn owl.

"You know how many names I have so far?" I asked Bobby.

"Names?"

"Sixty-seven."

"Sixty-seven what?"

"Names, Bobby! Are you listening or not? Aunts, grandparents, cousins, in-laws, whatever. Any relative I can remember ever meeting."

"Damn, Cassandra. You really are crazy, you know that? What the fuck are you doing that for?"

"Think about it," I said. "I've only mentioned it six or seven hundred times."

"Oh yeah. Right. You got that reunion thing coming up."

I ordered another beer, drank it quickly.

And then I erupted. "Jesus Christ! He's barely in the grave. Why the fuck does this show have to go on? Who cares about a stupid family reunion now? I wish they had burned down the fucking Parkway Inn."

"Take it easy, girl. My family can be a drag, too. But I don't hate them."

"I didn't say I hated them, did I? I don't hate *them*, I hate everybody."

My tears came in a sudden torrent. Uncontrollable, wrenching sobs. People were staring. Oh Jesus, were they staring. What did they think? I knew I was humiliating Bobby, but I couldn't help myself. I hurt.

He sat there speechless as a brick. He's never going to forgive me, I thought. But then he reached over and pulled some paper napkins from the dispenser and handed them to me.

In another moment I quieted. Then I attempted to apologize to him, "Sorry. I'm so sorry. Must be some kind of delayed reaction." My voice was so low I'm sure he didn't hear a word.

"It's okay. You're okay now," he said at last. "Get another beer and drink it slow."

"No, no, I can't. I have to go. I've got snot on my face, right?"

"You do not, girl. Go on ahead. I'll see you later."

I climbed down from the bar stool and was out of there like a shot. I didn't even say so long.

I caught the southbound "B," the Jackson Park line, at the Harrison Station. Those scary electric sparks popped beneath the wheels of the car, flared up, and burned out like fireflies. I used the train's greasy window as a mirror. I double-checked the snot situation and then put on a little of the lipstick I'd been carrying in my purse since tenth grade.

Besides the weight and the glasses and the long-out-of-date shade of lipstick, I am going on twenty and I'm still a virgin. It makes me sick.

The train emerged from the tunnel onto the blackened elevated tracks that cut through the South Side, straight on to the Jackson Park terminus. End of the line, no joke. I often tried to imagine the scraggly area as the glorious pavilion it had been in 1893, at the World Columbian Fair. They called it the White City, which amused me no end.

The el snaked along past old buildings with blown-out windows, leaning into the rusty curves like an old speed skater. One day, I always thought, one day this goddamn train is going to fall and I'm going down with it. I'd have given anything to be back in the Yacht Club with Bobby rather than heading to the family party.

I had been in the Yacht Club last week, too—the day after King was assassinated. Usually that dive pulsed from ten A.M. to closing with students, teachers, shoppers, and blue-collar drunks. But that afternoon, the day after the murder, Bobby and I were two of only a handful of patrons. We sat next to each other, talking low, not talking at all, swallowing tears and no-name brown ale.

"Martin was no longer effective," Bobby pronounced. "But that didn't stop him from being beautiful. He was still beautiful."

I nodded.

Somebody, clinging to the shadows in one of the booths at the rear, kept feeding coins into the jukebox. Over and over, they played the same two songs—"The Midnight Hour" and "Ode to Billy Joe."

Whenever I felt I had no place else to go, I set out for the college. Bobby and I had decided, independent of each other, to come to school that day. It was as if everybody else knew instinctively to stay behind closed doors. Ivy and Woody were sitting numbly in their bedroom with the TV on when I slipped out.

That April day had been pleasantly bright and quiet, like the end of the world. I rode downtown virtually alone on the Michigan Avenue bus. No traffic. Stores shuttered. The occasional passerby with a death mask for a face. Doom in the air.

The corridors of the college were deserted; all classes canceled, said the handwritten note on the main entrance. I stood in the deserted lobby feeling, and I knew, looking, utterly lost. I sent up a prayer of thanks when Bobby appeared on the stairs. He looked sleepless, unwashed. Without speaking, we left the building and turned into the Yacht Club next door. One pitcher of beer after another. One cigarette after another. We made bitter jokes and used the ugliest curse words we knew. We stayed in the bar drinking all day and into the night.

If the novels and movies hadn't been lying to me, Bobby

and I were supposed to spend that night together. Both of us hurt and furious, paralyzed and mourning. If there was ever a time for us to go off somewhere and make love, that night was it. But we didn't. By nightfall the city had gone up in flames. North Side, West Side, and South, the dense, rotting neighborhoods burned. The ghettoes—that dumbass word that so rankled and yet was indisputably appropriate— they burned. As if the bloody Negro past itself were being incinerated.

Eventually the fires were quelled and city life started again. So did school. In lit class we picked up Emma Bovary right where we left her; I went back to my standard lunches of grilled cheese sandwiches and sweet rolls in the cafeteria; and the much adored history professor, Daniel Bluestein, lectured us on Emma Goldman and gave high marks to the paper I wrote on the Soviet underground press.

"Cass. There you are. Come here and hug me. Don't you look . . . ah . . . devil may care."

It was only then, when Aunt Ivy used that phrase, that I remembered: I should have changed before coming to the party.

I was in a washed-out floral Indian print top, my trusty bell bottoms, and big, road-soiled work boots. Ivy wore a navy blue frock at exactly the fashionable length, just above her dimpled knees. At age—what?—fifty-six? fifty-eight?—she was a size eight with a minuscule waist, gorgeous skin, slender arms and hands, and beautifully tapered legs without a single visible mark, let alone a varicose vein.

She brushed a few wild strands of hair back from my face and planted a loving kiss on my brow. Then she interlaced her fingers with mine and just stood there looking at me while I blushed helplessly.

Ivy's eyes were gray—kind, but strangely opaque. When I was little I thought she could see in the dark like the patchy old tom cat to whom my grandmother would occasionally toss a scrap of food.

Ivy and Woody were not the typical mom and dad. I didn't have many friends whose parents could be a source of comparison, but it didn't take me long to realize just how different Ivy and Woody were. Not knowing thing one about raising a kid, let alone a melancholy preadolescent, they were constantly improvising. They spoiled me rotten in some ways. It was glorious. Getting over on them became so easy I got bored with it.

Ivy, with her infallible manners, unfailing tact, and matching good taste, made a lady of me, more or less. At least I'd know how to behave like one if the situation ever arose.

She took my arm and walked with me into the main room. Ordinarily dozens of decked-out relations, young and old from near and far, would be half in the bag and seriously partying at this stage of the annual get-together. Tonight, I could count the attendees using my fingers and toes.

The hall was like the waiting room at a cancer clinic. No one dancing to the live music that Woody had arranged at no small cost to himself. Nor were there any welcoming smiles on the few faces I did see.

"Not very festive, is it?" Ivy said. Tears gathered at the bottom rims of her eyes.

"Why go through with it?" I asked, trying not to sound too testy. "I mean—" I stopped there and gestured at the huge, underpopulated room.

"I know. But we decided it was too late to call it off. Besides, it might be the best thing, Woody said, to have the whole family together at a time like this. People need to know they still have family, something to count on even when the worst thing in the world happens. We may be laid low but we are not afraid. We're going to move forward, no matter what."

A stirring speech. But if those words had come out of my uncle's mouth, I was Lois Lane. No, those were her sentiments. Bet on it. She had convinced Woody to go ahead with the plan, and convinced herself of that rah-rah-we-shall-overcome bullshit.

"Have something to eat, Cass," she said. "Unless you're on a diet."

"I'm not on a diet, Ivy."

I checked out her weird eyes again. She wasn't crying and she didn't look afraid. She looked grief stricken and maybe a little crazy. Before I could speak again, she turned on her heel and walked off.

I made a circle around the buffet table, taking in the bounty: turkeys, hams, chickens, rolls, cornbread, every variety of white and sweet potato known to man, macaroni and cheese, fresh tomatoes, collards, fruit cobblers, coconut, chocolate and yellow cakes, cheeses, melons, berries, candies.

I had a sudden flash of memory. When I was thirteen or so, I got up very early one morning and stole into the kitchen. We had had a cream pie for dessert the previous night and I couldn't stop thinking about it. Ivy switched on the light and caught me reaming out the pie plate with my finger. I felt like the worst kind of pervert.

An old man in his wheelchair propelled himself up to the table just then. The young girl walking alongside him fixed a plate and handed it to him. They rolled away again, all without saying a word. Not very festive. Ain't that the truth.

My big white plate was still empty.

"So, Cass, I see you made it."

I gave Woody a quick kiss. "Yeah, here I am."

He always smelled of lime-scented aftershave, tobacco, and laundry starch. Tall and bony with features sharp as granite, he could easily be riding shotgun on the running board of one of those old cars in a James Cagney movie. Dark and sexy in a pinstripe suit. Slicked-back hair with none of the gray that now streaked through it. Someday, I'm going to ask Ivy how close she came to fainting the first time he kissed her.

They say that as you lay dying—if you're lucky, that is— you kind of relive all the beautiful things that graced your life. In my delirium, I'll be taking a walk on a Sunday afternoon with my Uncle Woody.

He never set foot in church, so he and I used to go exploring on Sunday until it was time to pick up Ivy from Calvary Methodist. After the three of us enjoyed a lingering lunch someplace, we'd walk home through the deserted University of Chicago campus.

Uncle Woody had the same awestruck respect for education that so many elder blacks did. And like them, he had had little formal schooling himself. The very definition of a self-taught man, he'd no doubt picked up his insistence on life's finer things from his early experiences as a waiter, valet, chauffeur, and so on, to a series of wealthy white men now long dead.

Grandma Rosetta told me that Woody's sophistication arose from his work as a Pullman porter. But Ivy said that was nonsense, Woody had never been any such thing.

My grand-uncle Woodson Lisle had also been a collector

for a colored mobster, a bootlegger, a hired hand for generations of dirty Chicago politicians, the mastermind behind the
booming policy racket, the moneyman in a long-established
illegal betting parlor.

So it was said.

There was no way, really, to separate the apocrypha
from the reality and Woody never confirmed nor denied any
of it.

Back on the streets of the neighborhood where Woody
had once lived, he was still talked about. Though he and Ivy
had long ago moved out and up to the Bellingham Apartment Hotel in Hyde Park, people from the old neighborhood
still sometimes brought their burdens to his door.

He was their last and sometimes only hope for raising
money for a wayward son's bail, sending a young girl down
South for the term of her pregnancy, obtaining a bank loan
for house repairs.

"Your aunt's not happy," he said. And that was about the
extent of his comments on the party.

Made sense. There didn't seem to be a lot else to say. This
was obviously the least well-attended family do in the
reunion's twenty-year history. As dumb an idea as I thought
it was to have the party, I was sorry for Woody and Ivy.
They'd gone to a great deal of expense.

Eventually I did help my plate. I could barely taste the

food, though. So I scraped it all into the nearest bin and went over to the open bar where I asked for a beer.

Feeling a tug on the back of my shirt, I turned to see who it was. Well, now, this was another record breaker.

"Hero," I said. "What are you doing here?" I didn't mean that the way it came out. Uncle Hero was a family member, but I wouldn't expect to see him here even in the best of times.

The sunken-eyed man stood there taking me in, a shy kind of smile on his lips. "How you doing, Cass?"

"All right."

"You looking good."

"Thanks. You look—it's great to see you, too." Okay. So there. We'd lied to each other.

Richie Lisle—known around the old neighborhood as Hero—was Woody's nephew, the son of Woody's oldest brother. In all the years of the Lisle reunions he had never once attended. More or less a contemporary of my mother's, he'd known me since I was a baby, and at one time I had hopes for him as a kind of big brother. That didn't work out. Now that he was grown, he and I had an uneasy, arms-length relationship. Even so, I pitied him for what his life might have been.

He had served with distinction in Korea, earning enough ribbons and stars to fill a pawn shop display case. We all knew the story of how, bleeding and hobbled, he rescued two fellow marines without regard for his own life.

But when that war ended he came home to Chicago, to Forest Street and the hundred others like it, and then life really got tough for him. For a while, Richie the hero wasn't allowed to pay for a drink. He began college on the GI bill but soon dropped out. His running buddies were no longer the young men he'd grown up with in the neighborhood but slick characters that his mother never ceased warning him against. Eventually Hero stopped inviting his friends into his parents' home. He had become a ferocious consumer of heroin.

It took the all-too-common toll on his faculties and wrought some changes that no one could have predicted. He survived through petty theft and housebreaking, a gig here and there washing dishes or bellhopping at downtown hotels. But mostly he lived off his elderly parents. They nursed him when he was junk sick, pretended not to notice as he pilfered goods from the house. They attended to him, visited him in prison, rushed him to hospitals, prayed for him, and then they died within eight months of each other.

Desolate at the passing of his mother and father, Hero cracked up and was soon sent away to the state facility at Kankakee. He returned to the neighborhood overmedicated and haunted looking. The rumors circulated about what kind of horrors he had undergone. He'd been lobotomized, some said. Others maintained the doctors in the crazy house had weaned him off heroin, but he wasn't a *man* anymore.

Woody assumed responsibility for Hero. Scared and berated him. Put him to work as a messenger, driver, cleaner—whatever circumstances dictated—swabbing the halls in one of the small apartment buildings Woody owned or waiting behind the wheel for him while he collected rents or dropped in on one of the wealthy black politicians.

Hero was good-looking when he was a young man. I remember that. A small, wiry build, handsome, swift, coffee-colored, lovely brown hair. I searched his face for the last bits of recognizable life.

"You seen Woody, Cassandra?" He was fidgeting.

"A few minutes ago, I did."

"Where he at now?"

"Maybe the men's room. What's going on?"

"Somebody need to see him. They got a problem can't wait."

"Who?"

"Mr. Jackson, from around the way."

Woody was walking toward us by then, poker-faced.

"What is it, Richie?" he said. He always called Hero by his real name. I hope never to hear Woody say my name in that tone, which wasn't one of hatred but stony disdain.

"Woody, Mr. Jackson's outside waiting for you."

"Which Mr. Jackson is that?"

"Clay Jackson from over on Forest."

"What does he want?"

"He says it's an emergency."

Woody gestured with his head and Hero led the way out of the room, down the stairs, and outdoors. Uninvited, I followed them.

Clay Jackson was probably not that much older than Woody, but it sure looked like life had been a lot harder on him. His back was bent, his hair snow white.

"Good evening, Clay. Long time." Woody touched the older man rather tenderly on his shoulder and used his other hand to fish his cigarettes from his jacket. "Richie tells me you have an emergency."

"It's Lavelle, Mr. Woody. My granddaughter. I can't find her nowhere."

"You mean she left home—ran away?"

"No. She don't run nowhere excep' wit those niggers burned down the dime store last week. She was mostly home with me after they did it. But then my neighbor say he saw the police arrest her. He say she was on the street and wasn't doing nothing wrong. They just pick her up real fast, put her in the car, and cut out.

"I been trying to find her ever since. Wanna know where they got her so I could see 'bout her bail. But they tell me they don't have record of arresting no Lavelle Jackson.

21

By now they done let go all them niggers burning and loot-ing and acting a fool. But no Lavelle. Why would they keep her? Why they act like they don't know who she is?"

"When did this neighbor see her get picked up?" Woody asked.

"Four days ago. Something happened to her, Mr. Woody. I can feel it. They did something to Lavelle."

Woody watched the old man, who seemed to grow even more upset once he stopped talking.

"All right, Clay. You come inside a minute. Catch your breath, sit down and have a drink. I want to ask you some more questions. Richie can run you home when we're finished."

Woody held the door and allowed me to enter first. Then he guided Mr. Jackson through. We waited for Hero to step in as well.

"That's okay," he mumbled. "Ima wait for y'all down here."

He was speaking to Woody but not looking at him. Instead his eyes followed the stream of traffic on South Parkway.

Uncle Woody stationed Mr. Jackson on a bench near the pay phone. I'd Bogarded my way into the conference down-stairs. But I wasn't bold enough to crash this discussion. Reluctantly, I began to walk back into the banquet room.

"It's all right, Cassandra," Woody called to me. "Stay."

I didn't have to be asked twice.

"Clay, who was it that saw Lavelle being arrested?"

"Moe Pruitt. He live on the corner, second floor, right across from Pleasant's. That's where it happened."

Pleasant's Corner Grocery. Another artifact of my childhood. It was where I'd buy my candy when Grandma gave me a dime. Forest Street residents bought all their necessities at Pleasant's. It sounded as if the rioters had spared it.

"And what did Moe say exactly?" Woody asked.

"Say he saw Lavelle come out the store. Soon as she turn the corner a cop come out of nowhere and push her into the squad car."

"Did she fight with him? Scream?"

"No. Moe didn't say that."

"Clay, what kind of girl is Lavelle? You said she was running with the looters last week. Is she in with any of the gangs? She been in trouble with the law before?"

Jackson didn't answer. He clearly didn't want to meet Woody's eyes.

"Do you want to find her, man?" Woody said sharply. "You want my help finding her? 'Cause if you do, you better answer me. And answer me straight. Understand?"

The old man nodded. "I don't know everything Lavelle get up to. I tried to tell her, so many times. 'Watch who you go round with, girl.' I say, 'Lavelle, a woman can't run the streets like the men do. These niggers out here use you up before you twenty-one years old.' But I can't keep up with her. I'm too old. She might get up to trouble but she ain't a bad girl. I'd know if she was really bad. She don't have neither mother nor father living. Just me. And I'd know."

"So she has been in trouble."

"Once or twice."

"What for? She got a record?"

Jackson sighed.

My uncle's earlier kindly manner had dropped away. He was all business now. "What for, goddammit? Prostitution? Shoplifting?"

"Yeah, bof of those."

Woody lit another cigarette. "Give me Moe's telephone number."

"He don't have a phone."

"Any particular nigger Lavelle was running with?"

"I don't think so. If she do, she don't bring him around."

"Did she ever talk about her friends? Mention any of their names?"

"There mighta been somebody named Luther, I think. He called the house a couple of times."

"No last name?"

"No. Just Luther."

"What about girlfriends?"

"She sometime went out to see a gal she went to school with—June Barker."

"The Barker house is that old white one in the middle of the block," I said.

"Um hum, that's right," Clay confirmed. "June be Coleman Barker's granddaughter. God rest his soul. You and me and Barker come up together, remember? You was a couple of years behind us. My brother—"

Woody stopped him midreminiscence. "The Barker girl, does she live in the white house now?"

"Yes."

Woody was being curt with Mr. Jackson. But I understood why. The old man had to be reminded to stick to the facts, like they used to say on *Dragnet*.

TWO

Uncle Hero was at the wheel of Woody's dark blue Lincoln. Woody sat in front with him. I rode in back with Mr. Jackson.

"Moe don't get out the house much," Clay told us. "Arthur bother him so bad sometime he don't like to walk around."

"Who's Arthur?" I asked.

Distraught as he was, Mr. Jackson chuckled. "You just be glad you don't know him yet, young girl. Arthur what we call that rheumatic arthuritis."

Woody was smoking nonstop. The early evening breeze snatched at the smoke rising from his cigarette before it could waft back to me, goddammit. I wanted one, too, but Uncle Woody didn't like to see me smoking.

Hero was a good driver. We cruised past Washington Park, deserted now. In summer it was thick with black picknickers, toddlers with their sand buckets, the young, the old, and the vagrant.

The park greenery disappeared and suddenly we were in the thick of the Black Belt. Dirty avenues pulsing with life. Wrecked tenements hanging above us like black-eyed skulls laughing down at the living.

We were only a couple of blocks away from the Forest Street house I'd shared with my grandmother. I hadn't been back there for years. As Hero rolled along a stretch of boulevard hard hit by the riots, I could only gawk at the sea of charred wood and broken glass. I caught sight of the ripped canopy over the old ice cream parlor where Gran sometimes sent me for a pint of hand-packed Neapolitan. Left to my own devices I always bought the creamy flavor called New York.

I had the feeling that Uncle Woody didn't completely buy the story that Clay Jackson had related about the disappearance of his granddaughter. One part of it, though, was obviously true. The neighbor who claimed to have seen Lavelle Jackson being arrested did live directly across the street from Pleasant's Corner Grocery.

In my day people were just as likely to refer to the store

as Julius's Grocery as they were to call it by its official name. That was because an elderly Jew with that name was the proprietor back then. Up to her death Gran talked with sorrow and rage about the fifty dollars Julius the Jew had swindled her husband out of on the very day they moved into their home. Apparently my grandfather, who had just cashed his paycheck, paid for a bag of groceries with a fifty-dollar bill. Julius claimed it was only a five. Grandpa had a fit about it. But when the police were called, the dispute was settled in the store owner's favor. That had been my grandparents' welcome to Forest Street.

If memory served, the dingy gray building where Moe Pruitt lived was one of a couple of apartment buildings on the block where, as I'd once heard my grandmother put it, *notorious* things happened. But that could've meant any number of things: all-night card games that turned to violence, somebody selling stolen goods out the back door, or just a "loose" woman doing heads without a license.

Woody, Mr. Jackson, and I climbed the two flights together. Halfway up, Clay Jackson began shouting Moe's name.

Moe's friends had been calling him that for most of his life, Mr. Jackson explained, but Moses Pruitt was his real name.

The strong scent of snuff came rushing out of his place when the old man opened the door to us. Clay Jackson had told us he'd known Moe Pruitt for as long as he could remember, they were the best of friends. But now Moe looked right past him—not at Woody, but at me.

I had no memory of him, but he seemed to recognize me.

"Ain't Rosetta's gal your mama?" he asked, looking me over.

"Yes sir."

"Yeah, ain't seen you since your granma Rosetta's funeral. Lord. You a woman already. What's your name?"

"Cassandra."

"Um hum. A good-looking woman, too."

The old dog. His eyes were dancing. He ought to be ashamed. Still, it was the one and only time in my life a man had shown that kind of excitement over me.

Clay spoke sharply. "Moe, let us in, fool! Can't you see Mr. Woody standing here?"

We took seats at the cluttered kitchen table as Woody began his examination of Pruitt.

"Clay tells me you saw the police take Lavelle away."

"I sho did."

"You positive it was Lavelle?"

" 'Course I am. I knowed Lavelle all her life."

"Did it look like she knew the cop?"

"I don't know. He didn't give her time to say nothing. I just know she hadn't done nothing wrong. She can't have stole nothing from that store 'cause she was empty-handed. Fact, she wasn't even carrying her purse."

"Empty-handed," I repeated. "Are you sure about that?"

"Yeah. I seen it plain as day."

"And you're also sure she was coming out of the store, not going in?"

"Yes, I am."

"Do you know why Lavelle went into Pleasant's?" Woody asked Clay Jackson.

"To buy me some Postum and a couple of cigars. And we didn't have no milk in the house. I asked her to get some cereal, too."

"So she was shopping for you."

"That's right."

Woody and I were obviously thinking the same thing. I let him ask the question: "Then why wasn't she carrying anything when she came out of the store?"

Jackson thought about the question for a long moment. He never answered.

"Would you recognize the cop who put her in the squad car if you saw him again?" Woody asked Moe Pruitt.

"I might. But it wasn't no squad car."

"What?"

"Wasn't no regular police car. It was a Chevy. Tan."

"And the guy who put Lavelle in that car, he wasn't wearing a police uniform?"

"No."

"Then why do you say it was a cop who took her? How do you know?"

I'm sure the only reason Moe did not laugh outright was his healthy respect for Woody's temper. "I know what a bull look like after all this time, Mr. Woody. He don't have to be wearing no uniform. Besides, what other kind of white man gonna be parked on the streets round here after all the sand these niggers been raising? Ain't but a few white folks who'd have the nerve."

I got up and walked the five or six steps from the kitchen into the front room. I parted the stiff yellow curtains at the window and looked down onto the street.

The lights were burning in Pleasant's. Open for business.

The mottled-skinned man behind the counter eyed the three of us—Clay, Woody, and me—his gaze zeroing in on Woody. Did he recognize him? I couldn't tell.

He spoke to Mr. Jackson in a low, solicitous voice. "How you getting on, Clay? Anything turn up on Lavelle yet?"

"No, Shep, it ain't. This here Mr. Woody Lisle. He helping me look for her."

Shep's story jibed with Moe's, more or less—less, in fact. Shep hadn't seen Lavelle being picked up. He could report only that she had entered the store that evening and picked a few things off the shelf, but rather than bringing them up to the counter to pay for them, she left abruptly and without explanation. He had found a jar of instant coffee, a box of corn flakes, and a couple of other items in a pile near the freezer. Once the door closed behind Lavelle, he never saw her again.

"Sorry, Clay. Like I told you, I don't know what was wrong wit Lavelle that night. One minute she was getting her groceries, normal. Next thing I know, she running out that door."

Woody made a brief survey of the little store. There was the entrance on the boulevard and then a gated window that looked out on Forest Street. I looked across and up at Moe Pruitt's window. He was watching.

"Okay, Mr. Shepherd," Woody said. "Much obliged."

Shep took off his spectacles and polished them while he repeated how sorry he was about Clay's trouble. "But you know these youngsters. She probably show up tomorrow."

Woody didn't respond to that. But before we left, he bought a pack of Pall Malls.

He then sent Clay Jackson home telling him to try not to worry.

The party was decidedly over. By the time we returned to the Parkway Inn to pick up Aunt Ivy, she was all alone in the banquet hall, except for the red-uniformed men emptying ashtrays and sweeping the floor. On the long buffet tables the piles of Reynolds-wrapped platters looked like a space-age forest of mutant insects.

"My Lord," Ivy said. "I sent everybody home with a package. But it didn't even make a dent. What am I going to do with all this food, Woody?"

"Leave it, my love."

"You can't be serious."

"Leave it. These fellas cleaning up will put it to use."

"All right. If you say so. Cass, see if you can find a shopping bag somewhere. At least Hero can take some home with him."

I went off in search of the bag. But I couldn't help feeling it was a waste of time. I couldn't see the blade-thin Hero, on drugs or off, being interested in Ivy's leftovers. The truth was, I couldn't remember ever seeing him eat, period. A wicked fantasy image occurred to me as I roamed the hallways: Uncle Hero at the stove in the hovel or the crash pad or wherever the hell he lived, wearing an apron and a chef's cap, busy warming stuffed veal breast and Parker House rolls while his junkie friends lay zonked and lolling on a filthy mattress. But when he brings out the desserts, they all stampede. I could see him Road Runner flat with a cake knife in his hand. God, I have a cruel streak in me. The coconut cake I was wrapping up looked mighty good. Too bad I wasn't in the mood. Under normal circumstances I would have been all over that.

As we drove away from the inn, we were all silent. Night was falling and the streets seemed to empty instantaneously. A far cry from the usual tableau of colored folks out to get what they could from the night. Because of the curfew that had been imposed, only a few taverns remained open, and in the dusk their neon signs shimmered like lonely apparitions.

A few young people, all male, clearly planned to defy the curfew. In their red and orange trousers and their rayon dashikis, they walked boldly across the Lincoln's path.

We rounded a corner and Ivy gasped. I looked out and saw what had startled her: an army tank, a remnant of the uprising. She snatched me close to her side.

One of the guardsmen peered into the car and hefted his weapon. He didn't train it on us; he merely cuddled it, then watched as we rode on. Woody made a cluck of disgust. Ivy's frame was rigid, her eyes just as hard. Still, no one spoke.

I broke the silence. "Like my friend Bobby says, we're a colonized people. This is an occupation."

Hero muttered under his breath. You didn't have to hear what he said to know it was something vile.

In another few minutes we were back to the relative safety of the university-centered neighborhood where we lived. We parked at the nearby garage. Ivy and I said good night to Hero, then he and Woody exchanged a few words before they parted.

Upstairs in the apartment, I went into my room and closed the door behind me. I sat down at the desk and had a private cigarette.

When I joined my aunt and uncle in the living room later, she was drinking tea, he was halfway through a scotch, and they were deep in conversation about Clay Jackson and his missing granddaughter.

"We're going to help them, right, Woody?" I said. "Isn't there somebody at the precinct house you could call?"

"I could, yes. Thing is, you have to know who to talk to, who to trust. Speak to the wrong cracker cop and he'll just give me a line of bull. Tired as they are of niggers, a missing colored girl won't mean a damn thing to them, specially one with a record as a whore. I'll call a couple of people I know downtown. That's a much better bet."

"My God, I can just imagine how they treated Clay," Ivy said. "How could there be no record if the girl was arrested? No matter what she did, they'd have to do the paperwork."

Woody picked up his scotch. He smiled tightly and grunted before taking a sip.

"What is it?" she said. "Why do you make such a face?"

He didn't answer her.

I knew why he made that face. I asked, "What do you think they did to her, Woody?"

"I don't want to speculate. I'd rather make those calls first."

Now Ivy understood. I saw her shiver.

I reached for one of the Pall Malls on the glass-top table. Woody started in chastising me, but Ivy stopped him. "Let her have it," she commanded. "Stop pretending Cass is still a baby. If she's going to smoke, let her do it at home."

He shrugged and offered me his lighter.

That Pall Mall is one fucking strong smoke. A couple of drags and I was ready to put it out.

"Sweetheart," Woody said, turning to Ivy, "do you know that fella runs Julius's Grocery these days—I mean, Pleasant's?"

"I think I've seen him once or twice. Why?"

"I don't like his damn story. And I don't like him."

"Then neither do I," she said.

I was tired as hell and outside of the six or seven beers I'd consumed, I had taken in next to no nutrition all day. But with all that, I couldn't sleep. So I sat up in bed and tried to jot down a few words in my journal, as Professor Kittridge, my favorite English teacher, was always encouraging me to do. There was plenty to write about but somehow I couldn't get the words down on paper. It was too difficult to herd all my runaway thoughts, let alone organize them.

I got up, lit a cigarette, and turned the radio on low. A local deejay who had been immensely popular with the white teenagers five years ago was cracking some tired jokes about hippies and soap. On the soul music station the host cautioned his audience to *stay cool out there, baby,* and kept the funky music playing. The smoking bass guitars and the soul shouts didn't excite, though; they sounded thin and hollow and scary that night. They didn't make me want to dance, that's for sure.

The news report said there had been scattered violence on the West Side earlier in the evening. Most of the looting and destruction was over, but here and there fires kept breaking out.

Authorities said they were confident they could contain the damage.

Are they really? I thought. Good luck with that.

THREE

I said Hero was good behind the wheel, but he had nothing on Ivy. Man, that woman could drive. It was Woody who taught me how, but I think Ivy might have been able to give me that extra zap of self-confidence and panache. She keeps promising me my own wheels if I stay in school, if I graduate with honors—if I don't do anything foolhardy like get pregnant without benefit of a husband. Well, that's your basic piece of cake. Unless I've got it all wrong, you need to *have* a man before he can knock you up and abandon you.

Ivy parked just in front of the doorway to Pleasant's Grocery. Her gray Buick was one of very few cars on the street. I suspected that most of the neighborhood automobiles had been lost to the riot—the uprising, that is. Funny how things could divide over an ordinary word. People over thirty called it a riot. Younger folks always said "uprising."

In the more genteel days a bell tinkled whenever a customer entered the store. Not anymore. Ivy and I walked in unannounced and apparently surprised Shep, the grocer, who was busy with a telephone conversation. When he looked up and saw us he hung up at once—no good-bye, no explanation to whomever it was at the other end of the line.

"I guess you remember me from yesterday," I said.

"You the one came in here with Clay. How y'all doing?"

Ivy answered him. "Mr. Shepherd, I'm Ivy Lisle. We're well as can be expected, thank you. These are bad times. But when you come to think of it, we're lucky to be alive to fight another day. Don't you agree?"

Shep looked at her as if she were from Mars.

"Just think of what might have happened to your store, Mr. Shepherd," she continued. "You must feel blessed to still have your livelihood here."

"That's right, I been, uh, blessed."

Ivy smiled at him. "As you know, my husband and I are trying to help Mr. Jackson find his granddaughter."

"I know that. But I—"

"Mr. Shepherd, you are one of the last people to see the girl before she vanished."

He tried to interrupt again but she raised her voice

slightly and kept right on. "My husband and I have gone over and over your report of Lavelle's actions in the store, but there are a few things we simply can't make sense of."

"I can't help that. I told y'all—"

"I know. You're in the dark along with us. It's only that my husband is a lot less patient than I. You see, he's ready to involve the authorities."

"The who?"

"He's scheduled a meeting with some friends in the sheriff's department. He thinks it might be a good idea for them to come here and go over your premises the way they would any crime scene. They'll probably want you to come into the office to answer a few of their questions, too."

"I can't answer no—"

"I told my husband, I said, Mr. Shepherd has been so cooperative. I can't feature him objecting to a police search. He'll probably be glad to tell them whatever they want to know, even about any relationship he might have had with Lavelle. But you know what, Mr. Shepherd? I asked my husband to hold off for just a few hours. I said I would bet money that you have remembered a few more details about the day the girl disappeared. Isn't there just a bit more to the story that pops into your mind now?"

He threw her what was no doubt supposed to be his threatening look.

She sent it back to him, then put her handbag down on

the counter and drummed her fingers playfully on it. She looked ravishing that day in royal blue.

He knit his eyebrows. Thinking, presumably. Weighing things. I figured he'd asked around and been told that Uncle Woody was nobody to trifle with, that he had connections and wouldn't hesitate to train them on an enemy like a well-oiled rifle.

Shep's chest rose and fell with resentment. It was time to play or pay and he knew it. I flinched and took a step backward when I saw him reach under the counter and then bring his arm up jerkily.

No, it wasn't a gun he'd pulled out.

"Here," he said, slamming the object down on the countertop. It was a small gold ring with a red stone at its center. "Go on, take it."

Ivy picked the ring up, not really looking at it. "Tell it slowly," she instructed.

"All right. Lavelle came in here, same as I said. She took some groceries off the shelf and brought 'em up here to pay. She was just 'bout to go into her pocket. But then she say wait up a minute, she gone go back and get her some ice cream. She head back there to the freezer case, but while she was walking she looked out the window there. Then she go on back. Next thing I know, she was running out the front door.

"I didn't know what the hell was the matter with her. I waited for a while, see if she was coming back. I thought maybe she went home to get some more money or something. But no. When I went to put the stuff back up, I looked over at the freezer. There this ring was. Just sitting on top. I took it and put it up at the front, case she came back for it. Look like it might be worth—I mean—"

"We know what you mean," I said. "You were saving it for her."

"What was it she saw outside the window?" asked Ivy.

"How I know that? Could have been her mama for all I know. I was over here trying to take care of my business."

Ivy began to examine the ring then, taking her time.

"Speaking of my business," he said, "unless y'all plan on buying something, I guess we finished, huh?"

"Of course," Ivy said. "I can see what a busy man you are. We'll be leaving now. We're grateful for your help."

He bristled. "I hope you grateful enough to keep the damn sheriff outta here. I got a store to run."

As if on cue, two small children ran in with a note on unlined paper. The older one handed it to Shep and he began to fill the order.

"No wonder Woody didn't like him." Ivy laughed wearily. "Oh well. He wouldn't have got much for it. It's a very inexpensive stone." She handed the ring to me.

We left the car where it was and walked up Forest Street toward Clay Jackson's apartment.

"Cass, do you suppose one of these boys that Lavelle goes around with gave it to her?"

I was peering at the ring as we walked, running my finger along its surface. "I don't know. I'm looking at it up close now. There's writing on it, Ivy. This is a class ring."

"Can you read what it says?"

" 'Chester Arthur High School. 1953.' "

"Where on earth is that? Didn't Lavelle go to school right here at Bethune High?"

"I guess."

"No matter where she went to school, she couldn't possibly have been in the class of 1953. She's much too young."

"If a man did give it to her, maybe it was his class ring. You know, someone older."

"Maybe. But it's awfully small for a man's finger."

"You're right. She found it then? Or stole it?"

"Not a bad guess. Anyway, let's hope Clay recognizes it."

No go. Mr. Jackson could do nothing to clear up the questions about the ring. He'd never noticed Lavelle wearing any kind of ring and didn't even believe it was hers. I paged through the telephone book in Clay's kitchen but couldn't find a listing for a Chester Arthur High School anywhere in the city.

Ivy wanted to ease Clay's mind a bit, I knew. She was trying to give him some hope. But in fact we weren't making any real progress. The ring Lavelle left behind in Pleasant's provided no answers whatsoever; it only raised more questions.

We left Clay's place and Ivy went to pay a call on one of the elderly women on the block who had lost a grandson in Vietnam. It would only take a few minutes, she promised. I decided to wait for her in the car.

Forest Street was much like a small town. It had its general store, its decent families, its drunks, its secrets, its history. On the way back to the car, I walked the length of it, looking at the old houses I had walked past every day of my young life, before Ivy and Woody took me in. I used to wonder what went on in the darkened ones whose residents were so reclusive we didn't even know their names. And then there were the places with auras so nasty or sad, I didn't want to know about them.

Some of the anger from those days rose up in my throat, but I managed to push it down. I never lose sight of how lucky I was. Lucky my rage hadn't forced me to pick up a pipe and kill somebody with it; lucky that ball of hatred didn't implode and destroy me; lucky I hadn't had to go to a lousy high school like Bethune. Chance had plucked me out of the quicksand that would get hold of so many Forest Street children and suck them under.

And if the wheel hadn't turned the way it did? Would I have ended up a pregnant dropout at sixteen, another ADC mother? Well, there'd be at least one thing on the plus side of the ledger: I wouldn't be a twenty-year-old virgin. My life would be utterly different if I'd had a baby. No college. No concerts or travel or museums with my ersatz parents. No security. No lovely apartment on the lake. On the other hand, who is to say a baby of my own wouldn't bring me the happiness I can't seem to find in any of the wonderful things life had brought me? I might even have found a man to love and be with, somebody almost as good as Bobby.

I stopped in front of what had been my grandmother's house. Curious, in spite of myself. Who lived there now? The little patch of grass in front of the house was all brown. One spring, in an unusual moment of amity, Grandma and I had seeded it with daisies.

Before long, a shade went up in one of the top floor windows—Grandma's room—and a woman in a head scarf stared down at me, frowning. Just then I saw Ivy moving toward me. I hurried to meet her, and didn't look back.

FOUR

We met Woody for lunch at Chances 'R, a casual restaurant in the Hyde Park Mall. From the very first time Woody had taken me there, I was entranced. Peanut shells invariably covered the floor of the place, giving it what I thought of as a rustic, bohemian flair. At this distance I see how ridiculous it was to think of a joint like that as glamorous, but at age eleven Chances 'R was my version of the Copacabana, a place in New York City I knew about because of *I Love Lucy*. I remember gaping at a pair of college students drinking beer and kissing openly in one of the booths, until Ivy pulled my ear and reminded me it was impolite to stare.

While Ivy and I were in the old neighborhood, Woody

had been busy elsewhere. And now he needed a drink, he said—deserved a drink, is actually how he put it—because he'd spent the morning talking to some oily politician and a city detective about Lavelle. He had a pretty big store of favors he could call in and he held markers on both men. He and Ivy ordered vodka tonics and I had a beer with my ham sandwich.

Woody was making us laugh with one wry joke after another at the expense of his corrupt city hall acquaintances. But when Ivy brought him up to date on our trip to Pleasant's and the brief visit with Clay Jackson, his manner changed completely. He stopped joking and asked to see Lavelle's ring.

When I handed it over, he pocketed it quickly. For the remainder of the meal he was unusually quiet.

Ivy picked up on his mood swing, too, but she didn't question him. We finished eating and she suggested a stroll along the lakefront before going home. "Walkie-talkies," she said, "like old times. Let's all hold hands like we used to when Cass first came to us."

It was early afternoon. There weren't many other strollers at the Point, that rugged lookout on Lake Michigan. A beautiful spot, but at night notorious stuff happened there, too.

The walk did not have the soothing effect Ivy had counted on. By the time we came to sit on one of the old stone benches on the rocky promontory, Woody was no longer concealing his agitation.

"Listen, both of you," he said, as if we had to be told. We didn't. "At first I thought Clay Jackson was blowing this thing out of proportion. I figured his girl Lavelle was just caught stealing something, maybe she smart-mouthed one of those cracker cops and he decided to teach her a lesson. I even thought she might be laying up with some fella at his house. But I don't think that's it anymore. None of those things."

We looked at him expectantly.

"What I'm saying now is, maybe Lavelle is in bad trouble, worse even than—I'm saying we've done about everything we could. Clay's gotta get help from somebody else now."

"What?"

"You heard me, Cassandra. I do what I can for people back on Forest Street. But I got a life to live, too. Not to speak of you, young lady."

"What are you talking about, Woody?"

His shoulders were pulling back. Not a good sign. Our lord and master was riled. Woody was accustomed to indulging us, his ladies, ready to give us the moon, but with the understanding that when it came to our family life his word was law.

"I'm saying it's time you minded your own business,

girl. You have to go to school. Get yourself up and out. That is your only job. It's nice you want to help Clay Jackson, but him and his are not your problem."

I didn't understand. I was about to say so when Ivy silenced me with a gesture.

"Woody," she said gently, "you know as well as I do, Clay will get nowhere without help. He doesn't have anything like the resources we do. He can't handle this thing on his own. He can't."

"I didn't say he had to do it on his own, did I? Let him go to the police with this. That's what they're for."

"But that's the first thing he did, Woody," I cut in. "You're not making sense."

"Don't tell me I don't make sense, child. You may be a smart little thing but you don't know it all."

Ivy and I exchanged quick, confused glances. When I tried to protest, she stopped me again. "Cass, you hush now. We're going home. Your uncle and I will discuss this later."

I shot off the bench, furious. "Yeah, sure. I'm not a baby anymore, right? I have a right to express an opinion like the rest of the grown-ups. But when I do, it's 'hush up, Cass.'"

Woody also got to his feet. "You about to overstep yourself, Daisy Mae. You don't speak to your aunt like that."

When you feel yourself getting mad, take some deep breaths and weigh your words before you speak. How many times had Ivy told me that during those early years?

Inhale, exhale, inhale, exhale!

The three of us made the walk home without talking. We rode the elevator up to our floor in silence, too.

But after Woody closed the apartment door behind us, I turned to him, weighing my words, to be sure. I announced: "You're not being rational, Woody. But that is your prerogative. You and Ivy can abandon Clay Jackson if you want to. I'm going to help that old man. My friend Bobby says class divisions among the colonized are illusory. We are a people who can't afford to let the oppressors use our societal aspirations against us. I may be bourgeois, but I'm going to show solidarity with Clay Jackson and Lavelle. They're owed."

That weighed even more than I thought. Uncle Woody looked all crushed in.

FIVE

talked a good game. But I had no idea in hell how I was going to find Lavelle Jackson. None.

After I mouthed off like that on Saturday afternoon, it was a tense weekend between my surrogate parents and me. Sunday dinner was so horribly polite it hurt. Nervous energy to burn, I went crazy on leftover sweets.

Monday morning I awoke early, dressed, and got out of the apartment before Woody and Ivy came in to the kitchen for coffee. If my mind tended to wander a bit during economics class even on a good day, the lecture on that Monday went completely over my head. The prof knew I wasn't paying attention. He called on me twice and both times I sat there with my thumb firmly planted up my ass. Playing the part of class dummy didn't sit well with me. By lunchtime I was in a foul mood.

I met Bobby for a pizza in the Yacht Club. I was a nervous wreck and in bad need of somebody to talk to. But what I needed most was some sympathy. The thing was, he didn't seem to have much of that to spare. He was in a rotten head, too, acting almost as if I weren't there.

"Something's wrong with you," I said. "You look weird."

"I didn't sleep."

Bobby's voice was so rough I barely recognized it.

I watched him pick at the sausage on his pizza.

"What is the matter with you?" I demanded. Frankly, I resented him for being in an even worse state than I.

"Forget about it."

"What? Tell me."

"I said forget it, Cassandra. You don't need to know."

I laughed in derision. "What happened? Somebody missed her period?"

He waved me off.

"Oh," I said, "I get it. It's something to do with Root, isn't it?"

He didn't answer. But I knew I had hit it. I could tell by the way his head jerked up at the mention of the word.

Some of the black students at Debs had joined the Black

Panther Party—not near as many as claimed that they had—but a few. And lots of us collected food, donated bail money, supported boycotts, school breakfast programs, and other activities initiated by the Panthers.

The campus was rife with student groups, including the Black Students Union, SDS, Progressive Labor, anarchists, Buddhists, communists, pacifists, Jews for Jesus, Ethical Culturists, even one or two Young Republicans. Everything from bomb-making classes to Living Theater clones.

Root, however, the organization that Bobby was part of, held itself separate from all others. Nothing that any other group believed in or attempted to do was radical, or "down," enough for them. Bobby was tight lipped about their doings and the rest of the membership. Occasionally I'd see him in the company of one or another of his associates. They walked imperiously in the halls, usually wearing impenetrable dark glasses. One time in the cafeteria I spotted Bobby in a feverish conference with two other guys and he pretended not to see me. I once asked him if there were any female members of Root. Yes, he said, there were a few sisters. When I pressed further and asked whether they had a real voice in things, or whether they were just there to make coffee, open mail, and do the same with their legs, he became pissed off and accused me of spouting "that white women's lib shit."

On the whole, he treated me like he probably treated his old maid aunt: with a measure of respect and affection, but also with the solid conviction that I wouldn't understand the heavy stuff he was involved in—the stuff that mattered in the real world. No way would he discuss the details of the "work" that Root was about with a goody-goody bourgeois like me.

"Can I come to a meeting?" I asked. "I've read just as much Marx and Fanon as you have. Maybe I want to join."

"No way."

"Why?"

"Dig," he said, "it's for your own good."

It was standard practice for us to argue, Bobby gently putting me down for my underdeveloped militancy. But this was nothing like our usual good-natured interchange. He wasn't making fun of me for joining the film society. He wasn't scoffing at me for helping the Quaker draft counselors with leafleting. He just looked freaked out.

I reached over and touched his wrist and he nearly jumped out of his seat. "Jesus Christ, Bobby. Tell me what's wrong."

"Somebody died."

"Who?"

"Somebody I knew." He exploded then, almost convulsing as the words came out. "He was set up! The motherfuckers set him up. They killed him!"

"Who are you talking about? Someone in Root?"

"Don't ask me nothing else about it."

I pushed my beer over to his side of the table. "Are you in trouble with the police, man? Please tell me you're not involved with somebody getting killed."

He shook his head and finished what was in my glass.

"Listen to me, Bobby—"

"Cassandra!" He stopped me. "Who the fuck is *that*? What's he looking at you like that for?"

No idea what he meant, I followed his gaze to the bar. My uncle Hero was staring at us, hanging on our every word, it appeared. I was too startled to speak.

Hero wasn't much worse looking than most customers at the bar, but he was incontestably out of place. The bartender was looking nervously at him and he was attracting other glances as well. One woman sitting nearby placed a protective hand on her purse.

"Who is that?" Bobby repeated. "Is he some crazy narc or something?"

"Hardly. It's my uncle."

Hero finally stood up and came over to our table. I moved over on the seat to make room for him.

"I don't wanna sit down," he said.

"Hero, this is a friend of mine—Bobby Vaughan."

The two eyed each other. Uncle Hero nodded and mumbled "Hey."

I was just about to insist that Hero move his ass from the aisle and sit down when it occurred to me: whatever the explanation for his appearance here, it couldn't be good news.

"I need to tell you something," he said.

I moaned out loud. Something had happened to Woody or Ivy, I just knew it. A heart attack. Auto accident. One of them is dead. What if they're both dead?

"Woody say for you to go to Field's at three o'clock."

"Excuse me?"

"You suppose to go to Marshall Field's at three and wait by the haberdasher department."

"Wait for what?"

At that point Bobby propelled himself out of the booth. "I gotta go, Cassandra."

I tried to restrain him, grasping at his shirt, but he eluded my fingers. "I gotta go," he called back, then disappeared through the front door.

I turned back to Hero in exasperation. "Okay. Woody said I should go to Field's and wait at the men's department. What am I supposed to be waiting for?"

"He didn't tell me that. He just said be there at three and then come straight on home."

Anybody else giving me stupid instructions like these, I'd have thought they were playing a joke on me. But Hero, the former heroin addict and mental patient, had never been known for pranks. I knew he was telling the truth.

I paid the check and gathered my things.

Marshall Field's had always been known as a store for wealthy white folks. Only recently could a presentable-looking Negro get a job doing anything there other than running the elevator or running a vacuum cleaner after hours. The occasional black woman light enough to draw little attention to herself would be hired to work behind the counter in one of the out-of-the-way sections—notions, fabric, what have you. But that was about as high as black people could hope to rise. In fact, forget about working there, it was only since the advent of the civil rights movement that blacks even shopped there in any significant numbers. No, we weren't in Dixie, but stores and restaurants had their ways—countless ways—of making you feel unwelcome.

The less prestigious downtown emporiums—Carson Pirie Scott, Wieboldt's, Sears, and the eternally déclassé Goldblatt's—one by one, they had caved in to pressure earlier in the sixties and begun hiring Negroes for white-collar jobs; a really ambitious black family man might even land a commissioned sales position in home furnishings.

I didn't fit the picture of the typical Field's customer,

black or white. And I surely didn't look like a well-heeled suburban lady shopping for hubby. I started to understand what Hero must've felt like in the Yacht Club.

Woody, who in fact did shop here sometimes, was nowhere in sight. But, as instructed, I waited. I sniffed the tester bottles of aftershave and checked out the calfskin wallets. The salesman's eyes on me, I began to look casually through the array of conservative ties and pinstriped pajamas.

A white guy I took to be the store detective seemed mighty interested in me, too. Every time I looked up, he was staring at me. I began to rehearse what I'd say to him if he had the gall to tell me to move along. I'd draw myself up in imitation of Ivy in high dudgeon.

I was fully prepared to let loose a volley of haughty putdowns when he walked over to me. But then he spoke in a voice that was anything but hostile. "Cassandra?"

I looked at him, stunned. Well, clearly he wasn't the store detective. What had Woody done? Set me up on a blind date?

"Jack Klaus," he said. "I got a couple of things for your uncle."

I suppose the attention we were attracting was justified. A portly black hippie with a skinny, middle-age white guy in a navy blue business suit right off the rack at Robert Hall.

"You listening?"

"I'm listening," I said.

"Tell Woody I checked all the sector cars, all the holding pens, looked at the rolls for the past week. Nobody named Lavelle Jackson, or Lavelle anything, was picked up or booked anywhere in the city."

"Okay."

"But about the other thing, he was right. I checked the list of missing valuables. Sounds like that ring was hers."

"Whose? You mean Lavelle?"

"No, not Lavelle. Just tell Woody what I said: it looks like the ring was *hers*. Understand?"

"Yes."

"Nice to meet you. You don't remember my name, right?"

"Yeah, it's Jack—I mean, no. I don't know your name."

"Good."

He walked swiftly away from me and directly out the Wabash Avenue exit. I stood looking after him. As Bobby would say, *What the fuck?*

Still doing exactly as Hero had said I should, I headed home immediately. I didn't bother with the bus. I walked the two blocks to Michigan Avenue and spent the extra buck and a half on an Illinois Central ticket. I wanted to get home fast.

I bet many a crime victim has realized in hindsight, he shouldn't have taken the shortcut. I know I did.

I loved the IC. It was a fast, clean, and pleasant way to travel from the Loop to Hyde Park, if three times as expensive as public transportation.

I got off the train with maybe a dozen other passengers and walked down the old pebbled stone steps from the elevated tracks. When I reached the bottom, the curved handrail snagged the strap of my oversize shoulder bag. Or so I thought. It wasn't until I began to tug at it that I realized a burly young man's arm was entangled with the strap. It must've looked like we were doing the Twist.

Woody and Ivy and everybody else in Hyde Park as of late were talking about how bad things were getting in the neighborhood. Marauding black youngsters from the communities on the other side of the Midway were snatching bags right and left. One U of Chicago coed had been raped and her male companion shot. Youth gangs like the Egyptian Cobras and the Blackstone Rangers were running pretty wild, their crime sprees no longer confined to the south and west side neighborhoods that had spawned them.

But this guy tugging at my bag was no juvenile delinquent. And he didn't look like a junkie. He was too clear-eyed and healthy looking. Sweat was breaking out on his high, dark forehead. I opened my mouth to shout, but his big hand clamped over my lips.

And then all at once my legs were flying out from under me and he was dragging me behind the staircase. Broad daylight, a mere half block from home, and I was being mugged. Not just mugged. Snatched.

The other disembarking passengers had gone on their way, not noticing what was happening. It hit me that, with the train platform hanging over us, no one up on the platform above could see what was happening below.

He ripped at the front of my shirt and the cheap fabric turned to powder. That's when I screamed. And bit him. And started fighting back in earnest. My fierceness took the guy by surprise. That made two of us.

I am a fairly big girl. Not as strong as a man, but I am built like Grandma was, built for hard work, even if I don't do any. This fool could have taken the money and run, but he didn't. He was knocking me around for no good reason, and I resented the hell out of it. I began to fight him like a she cat. Using my nails. Scraping. Kicking. Gouging.

I got two things for my efforts: a sock in the face and the attention of a passerby. I heard an elderly man's frightened voice calling out for help.

With that, the assailant shoved me aside and took off with my bag. I staggered out from beneath the stairs in time to see him half a block up, cutting across traffic on Hyde Park Boulevard.

The man who helped me to my feet tried to convince me to wait for the police, but I wouldn't hear of it. I was scratched and hurting and shivering and I tasted blood between my front teeth. I just wanted to get home. I wanted my mommy.

SIX

She came running toward me. "Have mercy!"

"It's not as bad as it looks, Ivy."

She could barely catch her breath. "Cassandra, what happened?"

Woody came rushing out of the kitchen.

"I'm okay, I'm okay," I said, not knowing whose arms I wanted to fall into—hers or his. In the end I didn't do either. I held up a hand to stay each of them, straightened myself up, and said, "I was mugged."

"Where?" Woody demanded.

"Under the IC tracks. He got my bag, everything in it."

"Goddamn," he said, focused on my torn clothing. "Are you . . . anything else, baby?"

I shook my head.

Ivy was trying to get at my face with her handkerchief, but I kept fending her off.

"Cass, you are bleeding, girl. Now you put your damn hand down and let me take care of that."

I was only playing at being tough. Her stern command ended the act. I let her lead me into their bathroom and help me out of my shirt. Then she cleaned the scrapes on my hands and arms, loaded up the ice pack, and placed it against my burning cheek. It was only when she kissed my forehead and took her hairbrush to my head that I began to cry a little.

Okay. All better. I was washed and in clean clothes. Woody sat close to me and poured a little whiskey into my hot tea. He was being sweet, handling me gently, but I could tell he was seething.

"Lord, people act nasty these days," Ivy said. "It's getting so bad out there. But we're supposed to be in a safe place. Why can't we ever be safe?"

Woody looked at her with tenderness, and even a bit of impatience, but so much sadness.

"All right," I said gravely, pulling his attention back to

me. "Enough of this mysterious stuff, Woody. Who was that guy Klaus and what the hell is going on? What did he mean when he said the ring could be hers? If it doesn't belong to Lavelle, then whose is it?"

He sighed before he answered me. "It happened in the old neighborhood, eight or nine years ago. Over at the school—Champlain. I guess you don't recollect it."

What was he talking about? Of course I remembered Champlain Elementary School. All too well. It was the site of most of my torture as a child. I'd run home to Grandma only to be told I'd better learn how to stand up for myself.

"There was a young white gal over there," he continued. "One of the teachers. She was murdered one day. A terrible thing. It was all over the papers."

Right. That sounded familiar. Yeah, I was beginning to remember it. Eight or nine years ago. I was already living with Ivy and Woody by then, attending the beautiful little red brick school on Ellis, the integrated school founded nearly a hundred years ago by a group of Quakers.

"It was horrible," Ivy added. "She was ripped up, that poor girl."

Woody said, "Butchered, more like."

"God, yes, I remember it a little now. A kid at the school did it, right?"

"Yes," said Ivy quietly. "I'd almost forgotten it myself."

"His name was Quick," Woody said. "Eddie Lee Quick.

Bad luck for him, he was anything but quick. He was a big afflicted boy in one of those programs."

"Special Ed, you mean?"

"That's it," he said. "He lived on Vincennes. From a family of seven or eight children. Mother was a domestic."

"So what's the deal with the ring? And Klaus? And all the rest?"

"The teacher—Elizabeth Greevy. Her class ring was one of the things missing when they found her body. She went to a school called Chester Arthur High, somewhere back in Ohio."

"And that's the ring Lavelle Jackson had?"

"It looks that way."

"But how? What's she got to do with any of that?"

"We don't know that, do we?"

He looked over at Ivy, who picked up the narrative: "Eddie Lee Quick was a pretty unfortunate Negro, Cass. Big but not bright. He confessed to the rape and murder. The arrest, the trial, the conviction—all carried out with great speed. People wanted to get the black monster out of their midst as soon as possible. But some folks in the old neighborhood believed the child was railroaded. Number one, he had limited faculties. And number two . . ."

"Number two should really be number one," Woody said. "They beat a confession outta that boy, whipped him something shameful. Photographer took pictures of him at the arraignment. Rolled up his pant leg. You could still see where they'd used their sticks on him. I don't even want to repeat what all he told his people they did to him. The civil liberties folks got him a lawyer. But the cops sewed that case up tight. Fast and tight. And the judge wouldn't hear anything that made it sound like this boy just might be innocent. Jury gave him seventy-five years. He was fourteen."

I nodded. "What about Klaus? He one of the investigators on the case?"

"No. Jack Klaus and I go back a way. He's one of a handful of cops in this city I'd trust from here to the corner."

"He must owe you a big favor."

"He owes, I owe. That's not important now."

I borrowed one of Woody's powerhouse cigarettes. "Jesus. That's some story. There's more, though, isn't there?"

"Um hum. The homicide detectives on the case moved mountains to make sure Eddie Lee Quick went down for that murder. The *Banner* tried to mount some kind of investigation but nothing came of it."

The *Banner*, a weekly tabloid, had for generations been the Negro voice of Chicago and much more of the Midwest. Politically conservative as it was now, it had done valiant work earlier in the century, attacking Jim Crow and spearheading more pro-black strides than I'd ever know about.

"The *Banner* never found out the truth?"

"I don't know what they found out. But it seemed like

all the people who tried to look into it came to grief. Rumor was, they were paid off, threatened, or worse."

"Worse? You mean the cops had a reporter beaten, maybe even killed?"

"I told you, I don't know all that went on, Cassandra. I don't even know that the boy didn't in fact rape and kill that teacher like they said. Time went on and people forgot Eddie Quick. I just know that nobody who touched that case had clean hands, including the judge."

"Damn," I said. "No wonder you acted so weird when I showed you that ring."

The three of us sat in silence for a while, until I heard Woody say, "You look tired, baby. You should rest."

I assumed he was talking to me. He wasn't, though. I looked over at Ivy, who seemed to slump in her chair. That was about as old as I had ever seen her look.

"No," she said, her strong voice contradicting her body language. "I shouldn't rest. That's just it. We can't rest until we find that Jackson girl. She may be caught up in something awful, but she's still a child and she's still missing."

Missing.

Oh Christ. I had totally lost track of what had happened earlier in the day. I ran for the hall telephone.

Shit. Just as I feared. No answer.

Where the hell was Bobby?

SEVEN

"You're smoking!" I said, incredulous.

Ivy lit her cigarette and then pushed the glowing chrome cylinder back into its place on the dashboard. "Hush," she said, "I'm trying to think."

She slowed down as we drove past Pleasant's Grocery. We could see nothing inside.

The dirty white house where June Barker lived was in the exact center of the block. It had been a landmark for me when I was little. When I passed the Barker place, I knew exactly how many more steps I'd have to take before I reached Grandma's house. Coleman and Annie Barker, Woody's contemporaries, had raised three generations in that house. Both were dead now. Ivy parked in front of the house and we walked together up the old stairs.

Clay Jackson had told us that June Barker was Lavelle's good friend. Presumably she was the big-eyed girl looking at us through the sagging Venetian blinds in the front window. Maybe she recognized us and maybe not. Either way, she didn't look like our dropping by was going to make her day.

June paid Ivy the courtesy of saying hello when she let us in. She even called her *Miss* Ivy. As for me, I introduced myself and got a withering look of assessment. "Yeah, I remember you," she said.

Thousands of young black women live with no man but many children. Some let their kids run wild or neglect them altogether. Some girls remain behind closed doors all the day long—singly or in groups—watching soap operas and smoking one thing or another. On Forest Street, you sometimes see them on porches, drinking beer, chatting with the neighbors while these empty-eyed babies with boogers clogging their little noses bawl their lungs out and beat at their blankets.

Their opposite numbers are nothing short of neat freaks. Fanatical about their babies' appearance, they seem to spend the whole day bathing, grooming, and feeding their children.

I put June Barker in the latter group. In the playpen at the center of the front room were two baby girls, both screeching happily and both looking like new-bought dollies. No dirty diapers in sight. No stench of sour milk and baby poop. The room was shabby, but it was filled with tinkling, candy-colored mobiles and stuffed animals.

June's appearance was equally pulled together. A brightly colored housedress with starched collar was buttoned all the way up her solid front and her hair was in rigid plastic rollers standing like pink soldiers on the field of her scalp. She kept one eye on the children as she listened to Ivy's questions.

She didn't listen very long. "What you asking me all that stuff for?" she snapped. "Mr. Jackson say y'all are the ones supposed to be finding Lavelle. You so smart, go out and find her."

"We're trying to find her," Ivy answered. "You and Lavelle were close. We thought you might have an idea where she would go if she were hiding. If she were afraid of coming home."

"Lavelle not afraid of nothing."

"When did you last see her?"

"I don't know. Monday? Coulda been Monday or Tuesday last week."

Ivy's next question was interrupted by the ringing telephone. June rose abruptly to answer it. She pulled at the long phone cord and stepped into the next room, out of earshot.

"Y'all gone have to go," she announced at the end of her conversation.

"I'll talk fast," Ivy replied, not moving from her chair. "I understand Lavelle's been in trouble with the law."

June's mouth pursed. "So?"

"What for?" Ivy asked.

She didn't answer.

"Wasn't it for prostitution?"

"Yeah. So?"

"Have you been in the same kind of trouble, June?"

She didn't answer.

"You have been arrested yourself, haven't you?" That wasn't really a question.

"If you already know that, why ask?"

"Only to see if you'd tell me the truth, dear. Lavelle's grandfather says you and Lavelle were caught shoplifting. Have the two of you ever stolen any jewelry?"

"Like I'm gone tell you."

"Does Lavelle wear much jewelry? Anything in particular you recall? A ring, for instance."

"I don't know about no rings. She got a pearl necklace from ah old nigger she was with once. He said it belonged to his wife, who was dead."

"How long ago was that?"

"I don't know. Last year."

"And who was the old man?"

"How I know that? Lavelle been with a lot of men."

"Lavelle's grandfather told my husband that she had a man friend called Luther. Was he someone special to her? A boyfriend, I mean."

June laughed.

"Did I say something funny?" Ivy asked. "I often do, without even knowing it."

"No kidding."

"Do you know this Luther?"

"Yeah, I know him. He a real special friend."

"What are you saying, June? Who is he, a pimp? Does he take money from you and Lavelle?"

"I like to see him try to *take* my money. Nuffy get us dates sometimes and we pay him a little. Okay? Now, you all need to go. I got company coming."

"You know, June," Ivy said nicely, "I visited this house from time to time when your grandmother was alive. I can't even imagine her asking a guest to leave."

Our reluctant hostess didn't need to answer that remark. Based on the ugly look she gave us, I could have written her dialogue for her.

"Is that all, Miss Ivy?"

One of the little ones took up her mother's words and made a song of them. "All mess Ivy, all mess Ivy," the child squealed.

My aunt stood up then, walked over to the playpen, and

fondled the little girl's head. "Miss Ivy's leaving now, baby. Don't you fret." She turned back to June. "What was that you called Mr. Luther?"

"Nuffy. His name Luther James but he called Nuffy."

"I see. And where does he live?"

June put her hands up. "Wherever. I got no idea."

Ivy put on her gracious lady mask. "I want to thank you, June. I know what an interruption we've been."

I had hung back till now. It was Ivy's show. She was the one with the weight of age on her side, probably some kind of reminder of June's grandmother's authority in this house.

"We'll be in touch with you, June," I said.

"For what?"

"To tell you when we find your girl Lavelle. I know with her disappearing and all, you must be worried sick."

I wasn't in Ivy's league, but I had learned a thing or two about deadpan sarcasm.

We were nearly at the front door when we heard a clumping noise from upstairs. It sent a shiver up my back. Ivy and I both turned to the staircase ascending into blackness.

"That wouldn't by any chance be Mr. Nuffy up there, would it?" I asked.

"Hell, no," June answered, daring me to ask the obvious next question.

I knew I had no right to demand to know who she had

74

up there. I might have asked anyway, but a knock at the door stopped me. June didn't make a move. We stood in the hallway on one side of the door, the caller on the other side.

"You really did have guests coming," said Ivy. "Go ahead. Open the door. We know how to behave in front of company."

June gave a grunt of disgust and then threw open the door. A flat-faced, gray-haired man stood there with a pint bottle of scotch in his hands. He just about turned purple when he saw Ivy.

"Good morning, Clyde," she said.

He looked desperately from Ivy to June, June to me, and back to Ivy.

"We haven't seen you in such a long time," she said. "How are things with you and your family?"

No answer.

"Clyde Gamble, in all the years I've known you I've never seen you at a loss for words. By the way, this is my grand-niece Cassandra."

He managed a "How do." Poor guy.

We all stood there unmoving until a woman's voice rang out from above: "June, what the fuck's going on down there?"

"We'll be going along now," Ivy said. "You can tell the young lady her gentleman has arrived. By the way, did Lavelle work here, too?"

When June wouldn't answer, Ivy turned to Mr. Gamble. "What about you, Clyde? Did you ever come here courting Lavelle Jackson? I believe you know her grandpa, who's about your age."

June wrapped an arm around the man then and pulled him inside. "You leave him alone and stop messing in things none of your business, Miss Ivy. Lavelle worked upstairs once in a while but she was never with Gamble here. Okay? And don't be asking me who she *was* with, 'cause I don't remember. I'm about sick of y'all and I'm not answering nothing else. You understand what I'm saying?"

"Yes, dear," Ivy said, and then called over June's shoulder: "And Clyde, you give my regards to Viola."

The door slammed closed.

"You didn't seem very surprised," I said as we took the stairs down.

"I wasn't. Cass, you know I keep my ties in the old neighborhood," she said. "The Forest Street whorehouse is old news by now."

EIGHT

I looked in the Yacht Club first. Then the school cafeteria, the lounge, and the Black Students Union meeting room, where I wrote out a message in big letters and thumbtacked it on the crowded bulletin board: BOBBY VAUGHAN CALL ME ASAP. I NEED TO SPEAK TO YOU. —CASSANDRA. I checked the rooms where I knew his classes were held. I even hit a couple of the men's rooms. Bobby was nowhere to be found. I had been phoning him every hour on the hour at his place, and still no answer.

I had been ditching my classes like crazy the last week or so. So when I walked into Professor Kittridge's office, he made a big deal out of calling me "the errant scholar." He was being sarcastic, but I knew he wouldn't hold it against me that I'd been skipping his class. More than that, I knew he was genuinely glad to see me.

"Hey, Owen. I guess I ought to pick up the assignments I've missed."

"Sure. Have a seat."

Owen Kittridge was another of my unlikely friends. In fact the odds against the two of us becoming close were monumental—far greater than the odds of my getting to be friendly with Bobby. At least Bobby was black. Owen was not only white, not only ten or twelve years older than I, not only one of my teachers. He was a Southerner. The last son in a family boasting an unbroken line of sons who graduated from Yale.

In his family's long history, however, he was the first who did not return to the South to live. And that was only the beginning of the traditions he broke. It was just a guess, but I figured no other Kittridges back in bloody Georgia were the ferocious imbibers of grass and vodka that I knew Owen to be.

Another thing about Owen—he despised the South. If we could meet on no other ground, we had that in common. I'd never been down there, but I had the northern Negro's loathing for it as the wellspring of unspeakable suffering. I knew that old black folks waxed nostalgic about their homeland. But I didn't give a shit how blue the grass was or how sweet the watermelon, or any of the rest of that hokum. I wanted to see it blown off the map like the troops were eradicating hamlets in Vietnam.

Professor Kittridge and I hated the same people at Debs, teachers and students alike. We were both loners, both great at plotting lurid revenge scenarios. We both longed for and at the same time loathed our parents. I had no reason to think Owen was literally, shall I call it *untasted,* as I was; he was after all a man in his thirties. However, the heady cloud of sexual revolution was apparently passing over his head just as swiftly as it was moving over mine. We were both bitter about that, too.

Thankfully our commonality did not stop there, and thankfully it wasn't grounded only in the negative. I could talk to Owen all day, and it didn't matter whether we were discussing heartache or donuts or Italian movies. Bobby of course was completely confounded by my friendship with Professor Kittridge. It was one of any number of things about me that made him call me crazy.

I guess the worry on my face finally registered, because Owen left off kidding me and his smile faded. "Something's wrong," he said.

"Yeah."

I got up and closed the office door and again took a seat across from him. Then I told him the whole Lavelle Jackson story, knowing I could trust him with it. I told him my friend

Bobby was missing as well. But I took care to edit that story; no mention of anybody being set up or killed. If it turned out Bobby had some guilty knowledge of a murder, the last thing I wanted to do was go blabbing about it.

Owen knew about Root. Yes, even apolitical, pothead-in-the-clouds Owen was aware of Root, the same way lots of people at the university were aware that there was a black militant cadre with that name. But neither Owen nor any other white people had much of an idea what Root was about. And for that matter, neither did I. Bobby kept it that way.

Owen took off his glasses and set them aside.

"So the assassination of the most influential black leader on the planet, a race riot, military occupation, spiraling slaughter in Vietnam, the looming collapse of the university—all that's not exciting enough. You're so bored with current events you have to involve yourself with a kidnapping that may become a murder investigation. Does that about sum it up, Nancy Drew?"

"I wasn't looking for excitement, Owen. But somebody had to do something."

"Watch out. Don't end up as a character in a Paul Bowles story."

"Can you see me as a sex slave to a Moroccan mugwah?"

"Worse things could happen to a girl."

He had a point. Women in those tales regularly wound up in a world of trouble. But they usually managed to escape with their lives. In that respect, they fared better than the typical male in a Bowles plot. For instance, there was the fellow who was castrated and left to die in the desert.

NINE

Everybody knew about Uncle Hero. In his youth he'd had those spectacular successes in the military. Now, in his middle years—well, the life he lived now seemed too trifling to talk about in terms of success or failure. The consensus was that he'd wasted all his opportunities and just wasn't much of a man.

But that was no reason to hurt his feelings. I tried never to treat him like hired help, the way Woody did. And I tried not to treat him like a toothless dog you fed at the back door, as Ivy tended to do. My dealings with Hero were polite but distant, and I knew that he knew I didn't trust him any more than my aunt and uncle did.

In this one instance, though, Hero had managed to re-
deem himself. It took him no more than a day to track down
Lavelle Jackson's pimp. Apparently someone in Hero's old
clique of druggies knew Nuffy James and where he was
likely to be found.

Hero didn't talk much. When he did, he tended to
mumble. This was the second time I'd asked him, "He hangs
out *where*?" because I figured I just *couldn't* have heard him
right the first two times he named the bar where Nuffy was a
regular.

But there was no mistake. He'd said exactly what I
thought he'd said. "The place is called Puffo and Geneva's.
It's over by Indiana and Forty-first."

Puffo and Geneva's.

Lavelle's disappearance was no joke. But I couldn't help
it; when I heard the name of that bar for the third time, I
broke into helpless laughter. I was laughing all by myself,
though. Uncle Hero turned his eyes away and stared down
at the ground. Finally I pulled myself together.

He and I stood smoking on the sidewalk near the blue
Lincoln. We were waiting for Woody to come downstairs. Of
course, Ivy had insisted that she could handle interviewing
Nuffy. Maybe she was overestimating herself. I didn't know.
But, pass or fail, I sure wanted to be with her when she tried.
My aunt Ivy sitting across from a pimp, talking in that tea
party voice of hers? Yeah, I wanted to be there.

But Woody wasn't having it. I left the apartment to give them some privacy while she made one last-ditch effort to convince him that she would be all right with Nuffy. A bribe, a kiss, or just the stone wall of his will—he might have used any or all of those tactics on her. In the end, though, we all knew the answer would be no. She would be staying upstairs.

As for why he agreed to take me along, I had the feeling it was almost punitive on Woody's part. I had insisted he help the Jacksons, I had whined and threatened, pushed him to continue when he clearly didn't want to. Maybe he wanted me to take a long, hard look into the box of trouble I had pressured him into opening.

The ride was short. We parked a few doors up from the bar, which was in the shadow of the Jackson Park el tracks. It was bright midday but I had a sudden image of our surroundings in the middle of the night: a train shrieking by on the rusted metal overhead, broken neon sign in the window blinking obscenely, men and women inside talking too loud, signifying, raucous Negro laughter, laughter that could turn on a dime to argument, arguments heating up to the boil, quicksilver exchanges of cash or kisses or blows.

Woody wore a dark suit with a faint gray pinstripe. The fabric was so beautiful to the touch that I found myself hanging on to his arm as we traveled the thirty feet or so from the Lincoln to the bar's entrance.

The funk that rushed at us was like a living presence, a drunken host embracing newcomers at the party. Hero, who had led the way inside, pointed to a booth at the back and then suddenly peeled off. In two seconds he was lost in the knot of people at the bar.

Like something out of a bad Western, a couple of older men who recognized Woody mumbled deferentially to him and then made themselves scarce. Strangers in Dodge City, we were getting appraising eyes from both men and women as we strode steadily toward the rear. Woody cut his usual impressive figure: a tall black man with steely features in his custom-made finery. I had made the effort, too, wearing a long skirt and plain white blouse rather than my bell bottoms. But I heard somebody behind us ask, "What he doing with that hippie?"

Once again I had dressed inappropriately. Damn, black people were hard on me. Maybe one of these days I'd hit on some kind of wardrobe my people would approve of. I kept walking, shadowing Woody's steps.

He pulled out a barstool for me directly across from a table with three people. "Sit down here, Cass."

I settled myself between two men drinking whiskey with Schlitz chasers.

Woody walked over to the trio in the booth. "My name is Lisle," he said, and it sounded like a warning. "You're Luther James," he said, and it sounded like a judgment.

Nuffy James's chest was sunken beneath the chartreuse silk shirt he wore. Even though he was seated, he was plainly a lanky fellow. The scotch and soda on the table in front of him was fresh, full to the brim. He was coddling it with well-manicured hands.

Both women on the seat opposite his were smoking Salems. One of them, the one with straightened hair, showed a gold tooth when she smiled up at Woody, preening. The other woman, stick thin with an unkempt 'fro, didn't look up at all.

Nuffy gave Woody the once-over, then his lip curled slightly. "What's happening, old dude?"

"I'm just fine, Luther. How are you?"

He furrowed his brow in that telltale way, the emblematic gesture of the not-too-bright.

"Luther, I'm looking for a young lady."

Nuffy grinned and then pointed one of his long fingers in the direction of the two women.

"A different young lady," said Woody. "Lavelle Jackson."

"Who?"

"Lavelle Jackson. You know her as one of the whores you run over on Forest Street."

Straightened Hair packed up her cigarettes and matches and moved swiftly out of the booth. 'Fro didn't budge. She was trying hard to look uninterested. She was listening, though.

"Lavelle disappeared a few days ago. Her people're worried about her. Are you?"

"I'm worried about nothing, old dude. Specially you."

"Been a good year since you were inside for pandering, hasn't it, Luther?"

"You a goddamn nigger cop, ain't you?" Nuffy said.

"No."

"You ain't? Fuck you then."

"What's that you drinking there, Luther?"

"Say what?"

"Let me get the next one."

Woody tossed a folded bill on the table in front of Nuffy, who slipped it into his pants pocket without examining it. "All right, then," Woody said amiably. "Long as we're acting civilized with each other, why don't you move over so I can sit down."

Nuffy laughed in his face and said something I couldn't hear.

I didn't see it happen. I just heard Nuffy's sudden puppy yip of pain, and then he was holding his right wrist in his left hand. And Woody was sitting next to him.

"Ask your lady friend to excuse you for a few minutes, Luther."

I heard Nuffy's grunt of protest and then his choked voice as he told 'Fro to get lost. What the hell was Woody doing to him underneath the table? Did he have Nuffy's balls in a vise? Was he pointing a gun at his stomach?

'Fro left the table reluctantly and Woody motioned me over there to replace her on the torn leather seat.

"Luther, this is a real young lady," Woody said, "not one of your run-down heifers. I expect you to treat her accordingly."

"Hello, Luther," I said stupidly.

"Cass, you take that paper napkin over there and hand it to Mr. James. He hurt himself."

I took the damp square of paper from underneath 'Fro's abandoned beer bottle and passed it across to Nuffy. He applied it to his wrist and the white tissue immediately turned red.

Jesus, Woody had cut him. I kept trying to explain it to myself some other way. I didn't want to admit what was clearly the truth. My handsome, patient, loving Woody had cut this guy's wrist open and now he was speaking calmly to him.

"Smart businessman like you, Luther, I don't have to tell you time is money. But that's not all it is. Time can be your enemy, too. The more time that passes, the worse it looks for Lavelle. And now you're in the same boat. Longer we sit here, the more blood you lose."

Nuffy's face was gray with hatred and panic, yet he struggled to sound calm. "I done told you I don't know nothing about what happened to Lavelle."

"Tell me about her steady customers."

"What?"

"Regulars, Luther. The men you sell that girl's body to. Niggers that liked what they bought the last time and always ask for her."

"Lavelle don't work for me, man. I put her with somebody once in a while, but she got her own regulars."

"Like who?"

"Garrick."

"Garrick? Who do you mean? White man runs the hardware?"

"Yeah, him."

I had no idea who they were talking about.

"Who else?" Woody said.

"I don't know—couple of those country niggers on Forest moved up here from down South. And another white motherfucker. I don't know his name. I just saw Lavelle in his car once or twice."

"What kind of car was it?"

"How I know that?" His voice was rising in pitch, as though he might start shrieking at any minute.

"You don't remember whether it was light or dark?"

Nuffy's face was wet. "Ima remember whether you light or dark, motherfucker. You see if I don't. Next time I see you, Ima kill—"

He broke off there with a gasp. It convinced me my testicles-in-a-vise theory had to be correct.

Woody motioned with his head that I should rise; then he pulled sharply at Nuffy's collar.

When the two of them were on their feet I understood what had been going on out of my sight. Woody was holding the nastiest looking razor I had ever seen. It was pressed to Nuffy's midsection. The shiny shirt was parti-colored with blood. He was the one doing the bleeding, but my eyes rolled upward and for a second I thought I would faint.

"We're going to give Mr. James a ride," Woody said as we walked swiftly to the front of the bar.

Hero sat behind the wheel of the Lincoln, motor running. Woody put the wobbly Nuffy James on the front seat and then slid in beside him. I took my place on the backseat, speechless.

Again, though it was full light, I was imagining everything in darkness. White electrical bursts like Fourth of July sparklers showering down from the el tracks. Crazy female laughter in the air. A barrelhouse voice, as my grandmother called it. I heard music, too, ancient music. Blues music. A yakkety horn solo. The name of the song was "Honky Tonk." And for an instant I saw my mother dancing with a drink in her hand.

Then it was light again. But I was still somewhere in the past, still witnessing as a child. I was in Pleasant's, on one of my ice cream runs. When I left the store I looked across the street where an ambulance waited in front of the pool room. The white coats were carrying a man on a stretcher, his head swathed in bloody bandages. It was Hero.

The shock of it was enough to deliver me back to real time, the present. I sprang forward as Hero was pulling into traffic. I suppose I was going to ask him if what I'd just seen in that flash was real—had he really been hurt at the local pool room? But the bloody sight of Nuffy James's shirt stopped me. I sank back onto the seat.

I looked out at the old brick facade of the bar. Puffo & Geneva's the carefully lettered sign read in new yellow paint. And beneath that, in quotation marks, "I Like It Like That."

As a kid it was my understanding that if you were black you went to Cook County Hospital when you got sick. As far as I knew, every Negro in Chicago who wasn't from down South was born in Cook County. But Woody took Nuffy James to Provident Hospital. I watched from the car as he led him through the double doors of the emergency room.

"Hero?" It was the first time I had spoken since I was introduced to Nuffy at the bar.

"What?"

"Did you know Woody had that thing? Does he carry it with him all the time?"

He shot me a fast look in the rearview mirror, mumbled something.

I lit a cigarette and gave him one.

"Hero?"

"What?"

"Was Uncle Woody ever a criminal?"

"Woody been a lot of things. I don't know half of 'em."

"But what do you think? You think he's been in prison?"

"Woody don't pay me to think, do he?"

"Hero, I've been meaning to ask you something."

"What?"

"Did you know Lavelle Jackson?"

"Naw."

"What about June Barker? You know her?"

Another flick of his eyes at me in the mirror. "I don't know that much that goes on by Forest Street since your grandmama died. But I know about that house where June Barker stays. That don't mean I go there, though."

"You have a girlfriend, Hero?"

"Cassandra, what you asking me all this for?"

"Just curious."

"No, I don't have no girlfriend." He turned to face me then. "But since you getting in my business, I'll get in yours. What about *your* man? Where is he?"

I was riled for all of two seconds. I was about to answer, Wherever he is, he's no junkie and he's no forty-some-year-old errand boy.

But then my childish irritation vanished. He was only asking what he thought was a straightforward question. Not something meant to taunt or insult me. How could he know I had never had a man?

I was trying to get into his business; he was right. But that was only because it had occurred to me a few minutes ago that Hero might have some firsthand knowledge of the funky things some residents in the old neighborhood were into. After all, he wasn't that far outside of Nuffy James's social circle. I just thought maybe he'd tricked with Lavelle and was too ashamed to tell Woody about it.

"I don't have a man," I said simply.

"Too busy with your books, huh?"

"Yeah, that's right. Too busy."

We remained silent until Woody came striding back to the car. He opened the front passenger door and before he sat down he took out his oversize white kerchief and wiped Nuffy's blood from the seat. I heard him instruct Hero as to our next stop: we were heading back to the old neighborhood. Woody never once turned around to look at me.

TEN

The iron gates had been pried away from the store window and were hanging on their hinges. Cardboard and wood planks had replaced the glass in the front window. The damage to the facade of the building was considerable, but the place hadn't actually burned down. Hundreds of glass shards sparkled beneath our shoes. I stood beside Woody as he knocked on the door.

There appeared to be movement inside. But the shop door was locked. "Easy, Cass. Be careful," he warned me as we peered into the dimness.

The door suddenly jerked inward, almost sending Woody onto his face. A medium-build white man with sandy hair was standing in the doorway, a hammer in his fist. Woody righted himself, hardened into fighting stance. Facing off, their backs up like Halloween cats, each man waited for the other to make a move.

The white man finally broke the standoff. He gave Woody a severe look before speaking. "Go home, goddammit. Can't you see I'm closed?"

My uncle stood his ground. "We're not here to buy anything . . . Mr. Garrick, is it?"

The man gazed at him in confusion. Oh, boy, did I recognize that look. A white stranger finds himself or herself in an interchange with a well-spoken, well-dressed Negro. There isn't a hint of threat or deference in the black person's manner, just a sort of watchfulness. It can provoke a wide range of responses on the part of the white person, often as not a hostile one.

"I'm Carl Garrick, yeah. What do you want?"

"My name's Lisle, Mr. Garrick. If you'd answer a few questions it could save me a lot of time and trouble."

He clucked in annoyance and started to close the door again. "I'm not interested in your trouble."

Woody blocked him. "Look here, man. I'm serious. We might as well avoid involving the police."

"Police? What police? What are you—from the insurance company?" Garrick asked in disbelief.

"No. We're acting on behalf of a Mr. Clay Jackson,

whose granddaughter Lavelle is missing. I understand you and the young lady were acquainted."

Carl Garrick suddenly changed from a regular, living man to a wax figure.

"So you'll spare us a few minutes?"

He didn't say no, so we stepped inside.

But once we were there, Garrick regained his tongue. "Now, tell me again," he said, reaching for the tall can of Miller High Life on the counter. "Who the fuck are you?"

Woody let the words hang there in the burnt-smelling air. He hitched his left shoulder in his sleeve, an almost imperceptible movement.

No, I thought. No, no, no, unless he's gone crazy, he can't be getting that razor. Was he going to go for the throat this time? Woody had to know there would be consequences if he cut up this white man. "Distinguished Retired Negro Businessman to Receive Life in Prison." That would be the *Banner* headline.

I began to breathe again when Woody dropped his voice into the blasé tone he'd used with Luther James. "I see you've got quite a bit of fire loss here, Mr. Garrick. But I'm sure you'll be back in business soon."

"Are you stupid?" Garrick slumped onto a wooden stool. "This ain't no business I got here now. It's a junk heap. Take a look around."

I did, cautiously. It wasn't so easy to see with only a tin

lamp for light. There were nails and screws of every size on the floor. In the corner I saw the hulk of the upended cash register.

"Guess I got off easy," Garrick said. "Not that much anybody'd want to take from a hardware. Lucky I don't sell spareribs, huh. You see what the A&P looks like? Lucky I don't sell TVs and stuff, huh. Fella owns a place—or used to own a place—on Cottage Grove says he can't keep 'em on the shelves these days. Yeah, all them hi-fis were flying out his store. Only he don't have a dime to show for it." He had a long, acrid laugh. "Jesus Christ," he muttered. "Oh Jesus Christ."

We waited until he stopped saying Jesus Christ. It took a few minutes. "Why'd you do it?" he finally asked, sounding close to tears.

Woody and I looked at each other blankly.

"I gotta make a living like everybody else, right?" Garrick cried. "I mean, why me? I didn't kill King. Why me?"

I suppose it was an honest question. It sounded heartfelt.

I thought Woody would go nuts, being accused of looting this white man's ratty little shop. And being asked to explain why the residents had unloosed hell when MLK was murdered. But he didn't. Once again, he met Garrick's hysteria with nothing but cool.

"The coloreds . . . you never know what sets them off," he said with a shrug. "It's a damn shame."

"I treated your people good," Garrick answered, pushing out his chest. "You had no right—"

I couldn't take it anymore. "How did you treat Lavelle?" I said, nasty as I could possibly make it. "Did you treat her good, too? Or was that unnecessary, since you paid for her?"

"What are you talking about? You don't know anything about Lavelle and me."

"No, I don't. Why don't you tell us about it. That's what we're here for."

"I don't have to tell you a goddamn thing. So what if she takes money for—for what she does? I like Lavelle and she likes me. The rest of it's none of your business."

"You liked her, did you? Do you know anything about a gold ring she wore? Maybe she got it from you."

"I don't know what you're talking about. I didn't give her any ring."

"No, of course you didn't. It was just a cold exchange of money for flesh, right?"

"You shut up about us. Who do you think you are, anyway?"

"You don't have to concern yourself with that, Garrick," Woody cut in. "Lavelle Jackson is the only girl we're worried about. When did you last see her? Was she with you last Tuesday?"

"How the hell do I know what happened last Tuesday?

You got a goddamn nerve coming in here and grilling me like this. I'll tell you nothing until I know why you're asking."

"Because she was snatched off the street and nobody's heard from her since. No trace of her anywhere; it's starting to look like she could be dead. Is that plain enough for you?"

The red anger left Garrick's face all at once. He asked, like a child, "Is that the truth? Lavelle is—something happened to her?"

"I got no reason to lie about it," Woody said. "Answer the question."

He began to splutter. "Maybe I saw her Tuesday, maybe not. I don't remember."

"Where'd you usually spend your time with her?" I asked. "Here, in the back of the store? At the house up the block, or what? Did her pimp Luther provide a place?"

"Don't be stupid. I don't truck with that Afro-head bastard."

"Then where did the two of you go?"

"None of your— Look, I'm through answering questions."

"Why is that, Mr. Garrick?" I asked. "I thought you were fond of Lavelle. Don't you want to help us find her?"

"I'll help you go to hell. Come in here threatening me. You move your asses off my property or I'll show you who's going to 'involve' the police. You think the fucking police are gonna listen to *you*?"

Yes, there it was, that assured sense of entitlement. The old reliable hole card. And that profound annoyance at being forced to play it.

"If that girl turns up dead, Garrick," Woody said, "I'll make sure everybody knows what you were doing with her. That includes your family."

"Don't you even mention my family, you old black nigger fool."

"Yeah, I been waiting for that one. I imagine you must be feelin' pretty cornered now."

Garrick stood silent.

"For a minute there," I told him, "it sounded as if you cared whether Lavelle was dead or alive. I guess that's not really true."

"Outta here. Both of you. Now."

The Lincoln smelled of fried shrimp. Woody had had Hero make a run to White's, an institution in the Black Belt since the 1930s. I guess he thought one of their seafood dinners would placate Ivy, who was waiting for us at home.

I couldn't help wondering how things would have turned out if he'd let Ivy do the investigating. If nothing else, Nuffy

James would be a happier man right now. Sure, everything would've played out differently with Ivy in charge. She'd have had to stand for a lot of shit from both Nuffy and Garrick. But would we be returning home empty-handed? I mean, except for the shrimp.

ELEVEN

I was still searching for Bobby. I'd phoned him a good thirty thousand times in the past few days but never got an answer. Anyone trying to find me would have a fairly easy time of it. Just contact Woody and Ivy. But where did I go to find out about Bobby? Who would know if he was sick or in trouble? I could think of no one other than his comrades in Root.

Bobby's mother was dead. He had a married sister who lived someplace like Gary or Michigan City—one of those dismal, poverty-choked cities a short car trip from Chicago—but I didn't even recall her first name, let alone her married name. Besides, I thought I remembered him saying he didn't get along with his brother-in-law.

I called him my friend, but Bobby was real close-mouthed about his past, bordering on downright secretiveness. I knew he had a room on Vincennes in a widow lady's house, with kitchen privileges and his own telephone. I had taken up with him one day in the cafeteria, dropping my usual reticence and fear and all but demanding that he pay attention to me. It was like my attraction to Owen. Something in me counseled that he was a kindred spirit, no matter how many things seemed to argue against it. I didn't know if other people fell in love with their friends that way, but that is how it worked for me.

I spotted a guy at the water fountain way down at the other end of the hall. But I couldn't remember his name. I'd had a lousy night's sleep and my brain was about as responsive as a used car on a February morning.

He was one of Bobby's comrades from Root. On the chunky side, a neatly kept 'fro and beard, nowhere near as good-looking as Bobby, but then not that many men were. He was wearing a kind of modified dashiki over his corduroy trousers.

I wanted to call out to him but I couldn't remember his name. I began to run toward him, waving my arms in the air like a spastic. He didn't see me. And before I could reach him he had turned a corner and was lost to me.

I figured I may as well check in with Owen, as long as I was in the building. But the door to his office was locked and the lights were out. To the right of the door were half a dozen notes scotch-taped to the wall. One of them, signed by the English Department secretary, said that Professor Kittridge had the flu and was canceling classes for the day. I shrugged. Chances were fifty-fifty he was really ill. He could have just been too hung over to teach. Next to that announcement was another one—from Professor Woolsey, saying his class's papers were due by Friday.

Woolsey was the resident Melville specialist. I dreaded the day I'd have to take his class and write the requisite term paper on *Moby Dick*, which I'd already tried to read half a dozen times. But if I was going to graduate with a degree in English lit, there wasn't much chance of getting around it.

Melville. What was that reminding me of? Melville . . . Merwin . . . Marvin. Was that the name? No, not Marvin. *Melvin.*

That was Bobby's friend's name.

The door to the Root meeting room was locked and the thick construction paper taped over the glass window prevented anyone from looking in. I rattled the doorknob a few times and waited, but no dice.

The cafeteria was located on the mezzanine floor. I decided to go there and get coffee, sit and think what to do next. Most of the cafeteria food was slop. But they had a pecan sweet roll I had a genuine weakness for. I got on line.

The short-order cook was a toasty brown, thirtyish woman with a nice figure under her stained white apron. Yvonne—pronounced *Why-vonne*—was a strange combination of things. A lovely looking woman with a lightning temper and a mouth like the bottom of a toilet. I'd seen her cuss people out for requesting coleslaw instead of potato salad. Of course, on another afternoon, butter wouldn't melt in her mouth. "What you having today, sweetheart?" and "How's your classes going, baby?"—that sort of thing. One minute she'd be singing an old hymn as she flipped burgers, the next minute she'd make a sexual remark that would make de Sade faint. I understood that she was nuts, but she scared the living shit out of me.

I was halfway through my sweet roll when I saw Melvin settling in at a corner table. I picked up my stuff and rushed over to him.

"Where's Bobby Vaughan? Has something happened to him?"

I had interrupted him just as he was biting into a corned beef sandwich. I thought that alone explained the irritation on his face. I wasn't prepared for the profound hostility in his strangled-sounding voice. "Fuck off, you silly bitch."

I looked around quickly. No, no one else had heard him

speak. But that didn't matter, the words still pinned me in place, I was too hurt to move. I willed away the hurt, though, and asked him calmly, "Why on earth would you speak to me that way?"

He stared straight ahead and kept chewing.

It wasn't enough to treat me like a dog. Now he was going to pretend I didn't exist. Godamighty. What had I done to merit this kind of hatred? I stood there dumbly for another few seconds. What would Ivy do in this situation? There were ways to handle uncivil idiots. Why couldn't I think of one?

I couldn't. So I decided to do what women have been doing for centuries. I put my hand on my hip, threw back my head, more Yvonne than Ivy, and let loose the vilest stream of abuse I could summon up, in a voice loud enough to wake up Herman Melville. "I'm talking to you, mother-fucker!" I screamed. "What happened to Bobby!"

Melvin flew out of his chair and grabbed my wrists. "You crazy, girl? Sit the fuck down."

"Make up your mind, you stupid ass. You want me to fuck off or you want me to sit down? What's it going to be, Melvin?"

He tugged me toward him, hard. And when I tried to pull away, he flung me into a chair. Goddammit, if he thought I was going to just let him roll over me that way, he was mistaken. I had been manhandled and robbed too recently to let him get away with that. I took in a lungful of air for the bloodiest scream I could muster.

But then he pulled a switch on me. *"Please!"* he said, sounding like he knew the meaning of the word.

"What did you say?"

"Stop yelling—please! Anybody could be watching. You don't know what kind of trouble you asking for."

"Let go of me."

He released my hands then and we sat in hard-breathing silence until the rapt audience we had attracted lost interest in us. Then we both took cautious looks around the room. Damned if I knew what I was looking for. I hoped he did.

The Root office was almighty chaos. Like the rooms of most young males. There weren't any stinky gym shoes and abandoned jock straps lying around, though, nor any posters of half-naked starlets. Most of the chaos was made up of pamphlets and boxes overflowing with mimeographed position papers and the works of Fanon and Chairman Mao. The wall art featured Ali, Che, and Huey.

Melvin fumbled in the desk drawer until he found a book of matches. Then he lit a joint.

Down in the cafeteria I'd given him the benefit of the doubt. I agreed to stop making a scene, sit quietly until all eyes were off of us, and then follow him up to the office, where he would tell me what I wanted to know about Bobby.

He kept his word, more or less. He told me not what I wanted to know but what in his judgment I *needed* to know.

"What do you mean he's on 'assignment'?" I said. "Who do you think you are, James Bond?"

"I mean exactly what I said," Melvin blustered. "He's out of town on business and he's not available. You can't reach him."

"But what was he talking about, something about a setup? Somebody was set up and killed. Is he doing something dangerous?"

"Keep your voice down!"

"All right, all right. But what—"

"Look. You got nothing to do with Root business and you not owed any kind of explanation. Okay? I'm telling you what I'm telling you just to shut your mouth. You middle-class fools think everything is some kind of game. You better dig, baby, we not playing here. We're an oppressed people, okay?"

His hands were tensing and opening, tensing and opening, as though he was fighting the urge to make two nasty fists.

"Don't you call me a fool again."

"Aw, girl—"

"Don't call me that, either. My name is Cassandra."

"Yeah, sure it is," he said. Then he turned and scooped up a square of paper from the shelf behind him. It was the note I'd left for Bobby on the bulletin board at the BSU. I stood there as he ripped it in two and hurled it into the trash. "Don't leave no more messages for him. Brother Vaughan will call you when he calls you. Don't go around asking about him no more. And forget the fuck about anybody being killed. If you don't want him to get hurt, you'll do what I say."

"Hurt."

"That's right. Keep yourself from hurtin' too."

I felt the press of dread and loss against my chest. Melvin didn't need to worry about me taking him seriously; I realized now that whatever Root was involved in, it was no game. I thought about never seeing Bobby again. I thought about him, dead. Before I could stop myself, I was crying.

"What's wrong with you? Are you outta your mind?" Melvin asked. "I told you, he's just away. He's safe."

"How do I know you're telling me the truth?" I pleaded.

"Damn. All the sisters Bobby know . . . What the hell is he doing hooked up with you? You nothing like his usual thing."

"I'm not his goddamn thing. I'm his friend. Haven't you ever heard of a man liking a woman whether or not she was putting out for him?"

Melvin didn't get to answer that question. The door pushed in and a tall, light-skinned girl in jeans, tie-dyed top, and an orange Afro wig walked in. She had chiseled features and unearthly gimlet eyes.

"What's happening, Tanya?" he mumbled.

She looked from Melvin to me and then back to Melvin, and began a nasty a capella rendition of the Isley Brothers' "Who's That Lady?" Popping her fingers as she sang.

She was inviting him to share in the ridicule, but he just frowned and put a couple more inches of distance between us. "I guess you were just leaving," he said.

"When will I hear—"

"Yeah, that's cool," he cut me off. "We'll call you."

"Call her for what?" the girl asked.

I heard the lock click into place as soon as I cleared the doorway.

TWELVE

All the way to Hyde Park on the bus, I worried about Bobby and brooded over the way Melvin and that beautiful girl had treated me. When was I going to lose that KICK ME sign I wore around my neck? I looked down and noticed a grease stain on my blouse and then got so caught up in rubbing at it that I nearly missed my stop.

As my functional wardrobe proved, I wasn't much of a shopper. Ivy, on the other hand, loved it. She could make a real occasion out of buying a pair of stockings and dime-store dress shields. A legion of salesladies all over the city seemed to spend their days squirreling away special items in anticipation of her visits.

I, on the other hand, was the salesladies' nightmare. At the end of every summer, when we'd arrive home from this or that vacation, I knew what was in store for me over the next few days: the ordeal of buying new school clothes. Head to toe, I was hard to fit. Suffice it to say I felt blessed when bell bottom jeans and flowy shirts became the national youth costume.

Woody and I were supposed to pick Ivy up at the ladies boutique in the Hyde Park Shopping Mall and then the three of us were to go on to an early dinner at the Tropical Hut. We were on time, but Ivy was late. Which wasn't like her. The shop owner allowed me to use her phone. I tried Ivy at home, but there was no answer. When it got to be a good hour past the time we were due to meet, Woody began to worry.

We decided to go on to the restaurant and wait for her there. I refrained from ordering my standard beer and went instead for one of the fruity concoctions that packed a punch. Woody drank scotch and smoked. Something was amiss. We both knew it.

"I don't think I can eat anything, Woody. Let's go home," I said.

He nodded.

Just as he called the waitress over to ask for the check, a slender white man came in. He was heading for our table. It was Klaus. The tipster I'd met with in Marshall Field's. Last

I knew, he was telling me to strike him from my memory. So what was he doing here? Obviously he had some news on the Lavelle Jackson case. It must be important news, I thought, something really hot, or he wouldn't be hurrying like that.

He didn't mince words. "It's Ivy," is all he said.

He drove us to Cook County Hospital, siren wailing atop his two-tone. "I was calling all over town trying to find you. Just lucky I spotted Richie in the Lincoln. He said he was getting the car waxed while you were eating at Tropical Hut."

"How bad?" Woody asked.

"She's critical. Shotgun. She was on Forest Street, pulling out of a parking space. We got an anonymous call."

Woody made a sound like a cat choking.

It was as if red lights hadn't yet been invented. Klaus powered the car forward, more locomotive than Chevy.

Woody's legs would not hold him up for the first few seconds after he got out of the car. He was half blind with tears. I was too afraid to talk. I shook like an old woman trying to thread a needle.

Ivy was in surgery, and would be there for hours. When Woody pulled himself together sufficiently, he made a couple of telephone calls. Some old contact in the mayor's office was dispatching his personal physician to oversee Ivy's care, along with a private nurse to look after her during her recovery. Except, it was far from certain there would be one.

We were standing in the corridor, holding on to each other, when someone called his name.

Woody snapped to attention. He released my hand. The worry and grief on his face turned instantly to loathing. The man facing us bore an uncanny resemblance to Roy Wilkins, the civil rights leader, except he had a great deal more weight on him. He was carrying a huge bouquet of hothouse flowers, but they were no showier than his wide silk tie.

"What are you doing here?" Woody said. On the face of it, that was a simple question in plain English. But the simple words were overloaded with threat and hatred.

"I heard about Ivy, man. What you think—I'm here to see you?"

"You haven't seen her in thirty years and you not going to see her now. Ya hear me? Take your goddamn flowers and move the hell outta here."

The man snorted. "Still the iron man, huh? Still think you can whip any nigga in Chicago. Why don't you git off it, Woody. You old now, so am I. That shit's in the past." He looked over at me then, tipped the baby soft fedora he was wearing and said, "I'm sorry, young lady."

"You can dress up like a New Orleans fancy man," Woody said. "Ride around in back of that big car and all, countin' your money. But you still dirty 'round the collar, Waddell.

You still a dirty, cutthroat nigga don't care about nobody in the world but himself."

"Listen to yo'self, Woody. You forget where you come from, nigga? You think you better than I am? Don't you know in the old days, you talk to me like that, I'd a cut your throat and shot you three times before you hit the ground?"

I was gaping at the two of them in disbelief. What in God's name was happening? Who was this man?

"Cass," Woody said sharply, "turn away from this bastard. Go and sit down somewhere. I don't want you near him. He puts his hand on a woman, it turns her rotten inside."

I backed up, but there was no way I was leaving. Not now.

This Waddell suddenly became conciliatory. "Hey, Woody, look. Like I said before, we too old for this. You got Ivy to think about. I just want to tell you, I find out who gunned her, that's the end of the story. He's gone, no matter who he is. He's dead."

"You let me worry about that. And don't do no worrying about my wife either. It's about thirty years too late for you to worry about her."

So that's what it was about. This man had been Woody's romantic rival. That can't have been the whole story, not with the white-hot hatred they obviously still felt for each other, but Ivy was at the center of it. More stuff from the past I knew nothing about. More secrets. Sometimes it felt as if nothing and no one in the history of my family was what they seemed.

One of the surgeons appeared in the corridor then. He was heading for us. That put an end to Woody's confrontation with the other man.

"Mr. Lisle?" the doctor said.

We hung on the doctor's intake of breath. "She's gone? Is she gone?" Woody asked pitifully.

"No. But we need to prepare you for the possibility."

My strong, upright Woody fell against the wall then, crying like a baby. The doctor remained there talking to him for another few moments and then went back in the direction he'd come from.

I couldn't bring myself to look Woody in the face; I kept my eyes averted. When I finally did look up, he was mopping his eyes. But his old enemy was gone.

Well, now we knew. Ivy probably wasn't going to make it. Nothing to do but wait. We went into the visitors' lounge.

Woody looked half crazy. I realized he needed me to be a grown-up now, not a child. And I tried to be. But I couldn't keep up my end. Within an hour, I broke apart. Started wailing and rocking myself. He could do nothing to silence me. "It's my fault," I kept shouting. "It's all because of me. You didn't want any part of it but I made you. I made both of you do it."

He tried to assure me that what had happened to Ivy wasn't my fault, but he couldn't muster up much conviction. No reason he should. Our nosing around, questioning people about Lavelle, threatening them, had brought this on. He knew it as well as I did.

I had the sensation that I was spinning and if someone didn't hold me down I would take off into space. The both of us crying helplessly now.

"I can't," I said at last.

He had his arms around me. "Can't what, Cass?"

"I can't bear it anymore. I can't be here when . . . I've got to get out of your life. You should never have taken me in. I'm poison, Woody."

"Stop that talk, girl."

"No!" I jerked out of his embrace. "Stay and be with Ivy. I can't do it. I just can't. I hope I die."

I took off, tore through the corridor, past the emergency room, and out into the night. Across oncoming traffic. I didn't stop running until my lungs gave out. By then I was almost in the Loop.

Sometimes in the Chicago winter your feet get so cold, so frozen, all you can do is plod. You feel as if you're wearing Frankenstein shoes. It wasn't at all cold now. The weather was soft. But I fell into a Frankenstein gait around the time I reached Roosevelt Road. My body was on empty, but somehow I kept going. I suppose I was waiting for my heart to give out, too. It was okay if it just burst. I'd die on my feet and in the morning they could sweep me up with the rest of the trash they don't let the tourists see on North Michigan Avenue.

Grant Park was on my right. And Debs College on my left. I turned into the building. The guard on duty knew me by sight. He was a sweet old black man in a faded uniform who was never without his AM radio. He said good evening but I don't know if I answered him. The strains of Engelbert Humperdinck's latest hit followed me as far as the cafeteria, which was closed. But the library was still open. I bypassed it and went to Owen's office, just on the thin chance he was working late. Naturally it was locked.

I sat on the nearby stairs and let loose all the grief I had in me. I was weeping out of guilt, out of loneliness, out of self-loathing, knowing that every piece of bad luck and every abandonment that had befallen me in life was my fault. I hated my skin; I hated the phantom who was my father and the absent woman who gave birth to me. I sobbed until my whole system felt dried out. And maybe I did a bit of praying along with the sobbing. At the end of it, I was mighty weary.

I finally got to my feet. I'd had no food all day, only that drink in the Tropical Hut. It felt as though my stomach were eating itself. Outside of the locked cafeteria there was a bank of soda and candy machines. I stood in front of one of them, staring. I'd realized I had no quarters in my pocket. So I looked at the Milky Ways and the salted nuts and the Diet Pepsis, trying to taste them.

"What's the matter with you now?"

I fell against the machine, startled.

"What's wrong with you?" he demanded. Melvin. Bobby's Root colleague.

"Hungry," I managed to get out. And before he could stop me, before I could stop myself, I was in his arms. Weeping all over again.

He helped me through the door of the Root office. I held on to him for all I was worth, my face buried in his faintly sour armpit. Not funk, really, just end-of-the-day salt.

There was only a bottle of lukewarm water in the office, and nothing at all to eat. I drank greedily. After that, he gave me a joint and left me to smoke it while he fetched a bag of peanuts and some paper towels that he had run under cool water.

When I was calm, he sat next to me on the old couch. I was still holding the joint. He picked up my hand, turned my palm in toward his face, and took a strong draw of the grass. His lips were wet against my fingers. "You all right now?"

"Yes," I said, but I looked away from him, embarrassed.

He took hold of my face, turned it back toward him.

Well, I had done it again. Through sheer doggedness of will, I had forced myself on a stranger, demanded he be my friend. *The kindness of strangers,* I thought, and even said it aloud.

"What?" he said.

"It doesn't matter."

He kissed me then, deep, and drew me closer. It didn't even occur to me until he was unhooking my bra that something momentous was taking place. First kiss—first kiss of that type, anyway. First time I'd wrapped my arms around a man in that giving kind of way.

I was ashamed of my lumpy body. I asked Melvin to turn off the overhead light. We faced each other naked in the dimness of the desk lamp. More kisses, and him guiding my hands as I touched him.

"I have to tell you something," I said, pushing away from him.

"What?"

"I never—I'm not—you may not want me. I never had sex before."

"You kidding."

"I'm sorry. I hear some men like that," I said, "and some don't."

Melvin surprised me in just about every way. I'd have guessed he was the kind who would *not* like being with a virgin. I'd have thought he would spend minimal time with preliminaries. And I would never have predicted he'd be so caring. Cassandra, the doomed little fuckup, had lucked out again. Less than twelve hours ago Melvin had been my nemesis, we'd nearly come to violence against each other. And now he was sweetly taking me, more sweetly, even, than in those old fantasies starring Bobby.

After we made love he found a rain poncho in one of the desk drawers and covered me with it. Then he held me while I told him the awful thing that had sent me running to school that night. He quieted me when I began to fret again, and he went on holding me while I napped.

He woke me in a gentle way, too. I could barely believe how he was making me feel, just with a few strokes of his fingers.

"I want to ask you something," I said a while later. "I promise I'm not going to nag you about Bobby. I just want to know why you didn't like me. Before, I mean. Like when I'd see you in the hall, or that time you all were sending stuff down South and I brought all the canned goods here to the office. You didn't know me at all, but you treated me like I was an asshole."

Maybe he thought if he sat there eating peanuts long enough, I'd forget the question. But I waited him out.

"Look, Cassandra," he said finally, "you not like I am."

"What do you mean?"

"I mean everything, everything about you. You talk different. You act different. Almost like you want to be white or something. You just not in the fight the way we are. You not down with niggers the way we are. You just not."

"Why? Because I don't wear the uniform? You know how many people wear a natural and talk jive but never lift a finger in their life to help other people? You think just because somebody puts on a dashiki, that means they're not full of shit? That's what it's about—the clothes you wear?"

"Hey, hey, cool it. I'm not saying none of that. I know jive niggers from the real thing. They ain't fooling nobody. I'm just telling you, you think you found some decent kind of way to act in the world and it's gonna do some good. It ain't, baby, it ain't."

"So if I want to do some good, I should be like you, right? You and Bobby are gonna kill and be killed . . . walk into setups . . . and I should think it's right on."

"Hey, we didn't declare war on the white man. He declared war on us. Way we figure, we either gonna fight this motherfucker or we not. Ain't a lot else to say about it."

Not true, I wanted to say. But I didn't; I shut up for a change. I lay there, casting Melvin and myself in an absurd version of some WW II movie, only with an all-black cast. Just before he ships out, soldier and girl next door have a night of love. A few days later, he's posted not to the Pacific but to Sixty-third Street and Cottage Grove, and instead of Japs, he's killing honkies with a grease gun. In the last scene he takes one in the head from a Chicago pig in reflector sunglasses.

The university shut down at eleven. We dressed and had a cigarette in the fifteen minutes remaining.

"Where you live at?" he asked when he had locked up.

"Hyde Park."

"Your people got money?"

"Some," I said. "But I can't go home now. I can't face my uncle."

"You gotta go somewhere. I can't take you home with me."

"Why not? Where do you live?"

He didn't answer.

Oh. A live-in girlfriend. Maybe even a wife. Or maybe it was just more secrecy bullshit.

"You still hungry?"

"Yes."

"I'd help you out, but I'm short. 'Bout the best I can do is give you some carfare. What you gone do?"

"I'll be okay. I'll spend the night with a friend."

We parted outside. He walked off in the direction of State Street. I stood on Michigan Avenue for a good five minutes, not moving one way or the other. Finally I crossed the avenue. I decided to take a bus.

I called Professor Kittridge from the street corner pay phone.

"Owen, do you really have the flu?" I asked when he picked up.

"Who is this?"

"Cassandra."

"Where are you? You sound strange."

"I need a place to be, just for the night."

"I'll come and get you."

"That's okay. I'm close."

Owen didn't live anyplace special. His was a typical white neighborhood on the North Side. Blue-collar families side by side with student-roommates, young marrieds, artists, underpaid academics. There were community savings banks and pancake houses and conveniently located supermarkets. The mail was delivered and the streets were swept, apartment building lobbies clean and well lit. A world away, in other words, from most of its west or south side counterparts.

One thing about the rigidly segregated city of Chicago— the block-busting system was amazingly efficient. We saw neighborhoods turn from all white to all black in less than sixty days. A working-class white neighborhood was by any rational standard a perfectly acceptable, normal place to live. The usual blue-collar community of Negroes had by the 1960s become a kind of carnival of violence and neglect with wildly unreliable city services or none at all.

I rang the bell marked "Kittridge." Now, here was another thing you rarely found in a poor black community: a buzzer that worked.

Nothing but a couple of limes and half a can of decaying Campbell's soup in Owen's refrigerator. He ordered a pizza for me. I didn't know what kind of topping it had and I didn't care. I had one Coke after another while he drank red wine.

"Your uncle must be worried about you," he said after I'd told him about Ivy and my freak-out at the hospital.

"I know, I know. I'll have to quit school and get out on my own if Ivy dies."

"What do you mean, you'll quit school?"

"If I have to. I don't know. Maybe I can go at night."

"It won't come to that, I'm sure."

"Why not? Thousands of people do it. Why should I be any different?"

"Because you're an excellent student and you won't be eligible to apply for the McConwill grant if you aren't full time."

I shrugged. "Then I guess I won't be eligible."

"You're going to give up, just like that? You're no longer interested in going to England?"

Interested was hardly the word. Up until the moment that cop told us that Ivy had been shotgunned, I would have done cartwheels if I won the McConwill scholarship. An all-expenses-paid year in England. I would actually get to live in Europe, maybe even see Paris.

But all that had changed. Detective Klaus changed it when he walked into the restaurant.

"It was some kind of omen," I said. "Ivy getting hurt, maybe dying, is horrible enough on its own. But it means something else. For me. It's a signal that I wasn't meant to get the things I want in life. It's a signal I was meant to be alone—that I just fuck up other people's lives when I try to change what was obviously meant to be."

Owen stopped me. "You're talking shit, my friend. You're tired and sad. That's all."

"And guilty."

"Did you hear me? You're talking shit. So stop talking and go to bed. The blanket's in the hall closet."

"There's something else, Owen."

"What?"

"I got laid."

"Tonight? You mean tonight?"

"Yes. I kind of bulldozed this guy Melvin into deflowering me."

Owen didn't appear to comprehend what I'd just said. More than that, he looked aghast. "Okay," he finally said. "Sleep now." And he headed off toward his bedroom.

"Wait a minute," I said.

He turned back, his face still clouded over.

"Owen, are you mad at me or something?"

"No. Of course not."

"Look. We both know if I were good-looking, either you or Bobby would have slept with me long ago."

"No, please don't. Don't say anymore now. We'll talk about it another time."

"All right."

But it wasn't. I lay on the sofa, fighting sleep. I didn't win.

THIRTEEN

I figured if the hospital switchboard operator put me through to the room, Ivy couldn't be dead. They wouldn't assign a phone number to a dead patient.

Woody picked up. I didn't speak for a few seconds.

"Cass? Is that you?"

"Yes."

"Where are you, baby?"

"At my professor's."

"Where? I'll send Hero to pick you up."

"How is she?"

"Bad. We just have to hope. Now give me that address."

"No, it's way north. The el is quicker."

"Come directly to the hospital, you hear? Take a taxi if you can get one."

"Yes sir."

"You all right, baby?"

"Yes."

I could have wept with relief. Ivy was still alive and Woody didn't hate me.

Owen made some terrible tasting coffee. I had one cup and then set out.

"Come back anytime you need to," he called from the top of the stairs.

"Thanks."

"Cassandra!"

I looked up.

"Nothing. Just let me know how you are."

"I'm sorry, Woody."

"I know you are, sugar."

My great-uncle smoothed my hair away from my face. I knew I looked a mess. His beautiful fingers, like black cigars, lingered on my forehead.

"Where is she?" I asked.

"Back in the operating room. They needed to check out some bleeding she had during the night."

"You mean she's worse?"

"I don't think so. They just have her in recovery for a while. She'll be back down."

No amount of coaxing could convince Woody to go home and get some rest. But around three in the afternoon, he pulled two chairs together and stretched out. Within minutes, he was asleep.

I went down to the newsstand looking to buy a *New Yorker*. No luck. I settled for *Ebony* and *Ellery Queen*. On the way out of the shop I passed the rack that held the copies of *Jet*. I had not been able to look at that particular magazine since I was six or seven years old. I was reading by then, and I had found a *Jet* in the living room of my grandmother's house. In it, I came upon a photograph of the murdered Emmett Till in all its horror. Every time I look at the cover of that magazine I see his caved-in skull behind my eyes. I hear his scorching shrieks of agony. And images of his tormentors—wet mouths, red faces—pelt my brain. Forever after, this to me is Mississippi.

Ivy was not returned to her room. They decided to keep her in Intensive Care for the rest of the day. I read, begged coffee from the nurses' station, wandered the halls of the hospital, took periodic trips outdoors to stand in the parking lot and smoke.

At seven o'clock Woody relented and said a good night's sleep would be the best thing for both of us. But first he'd have Hero drop us someplace where we could get a hot meal.

We settled on Shorty's, on Forty-third, where the smothered chicken and biscuits were legendary. Woody invited Hero to eat with us, but he declined. We left him in the Lincoln reading my copy of *Ebony*.

"Woody," I said carefully while we were waiting for our peach cobbler, "maybe it's not the best time—"

"Don't, baby," he interrupted. "I know what you want to know. You want to ask me about Henry Waddell. I'm sorry that happened while you were there."

"That's okay. But who is he? Somebody dangerous?"

He waited a minute before speaking. "Yes," he said simply.

"What was all that talk about thirty years ago? Was he interested in Ivy at the same time you were?"

He didn't answer.

"Was he her lover?"

"I'm not gonna talk about that. It's nothing you need to know about."

"All right. So that part's none of my business. But what about him being dangerous? He was some kind of crook, right?"

"Yeah, that he was. Still is. He and I tangled a lot way back when. It's a wonder one of us didn't kill the other."

"And you? What kind of stuff were you doing? Were you in the policy racket or something?"

"Cassandra, you're a young girl. You got no idea what a

Negro had to do to survive in this city forty years ago. I'm not proud of some of the things I did. But I never set out to do ill the way Henry Waddell did. I never caused the kind of misery he trades in with that dope. I never sucked the life out of poor niggers like he does with his loan-sharking. Like he said, we're both old now and the past is the past. And that's about all I'm gone tell you for now, Daisy Mae. You know that saying, Curiosity killed the cat."

"But maybe someday you will tell me more, right? Or Ivy might?"

"Eat your pie, Cass. We gotta get some sleep."

After the meal was finished, we stopped at the take-out counter and picked up an order of fried chicken for Hero, who was parked at the corner. Woody had a fatherly arm around my shoulders. We were talking about that long-postponed return trip to Ghana that Ivy wanted to take, when two men appeared out of nowhere.

It was my scream that brought Hero running out of the Lincoln.

One of the men used his fists to knock me down. The other had a baseball bat. He was aiming for Woody's head. Woody was quick enough to block the blow, but he lost his footing and went tumbling backward. By that time Hero had arrived. He jumped the big man with the bat from behind. I heard bones cracking and the big man went down in a heap. Hero had broken his neck.

The other man dragged me to my feet and used me as a shield while he backed away.

"Nigger, get your hands off that girl," Woody roared and lunged toward us, his blade shining like a new dime.

"Stay the fuck back," the guy commanded, and then the glint of his knife registered at the periphery of my vision. "I'll stick her ass."

Woody froze in his tracks. "You're a dead man if you do."

He had distracted the man just long enough for Hero to make a move. I went down hard, the grit of the pavement grinding into my knees. Hero and the man were like drunken waltzers as they battled for a grip on the knife. Woody moved in then, but too late. We saw the man push Hero off just enough to thrust the blade upward into his chest. Hero collapsed. And with that the man began to run, run faster than I could, and certainly three times as fast as Woody could.

Two men on the ground.

The last red life poured out of Uncle Hero's mouth and heart and his limbs were relaxing into the long flight ahead of him. But the muscular black man—the one who had mugged me under the train tracks—looked as if he'd been dead forever.

I began to moan and scream, like you do in any nightmare, and I ran blindly into the nearest bright light.

FOURTEEN

He had no wife, no children, no lover, no friends that we knew of. So where did all the mourners come from? I guess black people just gravitate to funerals.

Hero was a former marine who had drifted into drug abuse. His options in life, his social contacts, his ability to live, love, and work, had dwindled steadily until he was all but invisible. He was like a million other guys. Folks on the block who didn't have much use for them while they were alive turn up all weepy and shit at the funeral—out of respect for the parents, or because they recall how sweet those no-count men had been as babies, and especially how much their mamas had loved them.

I had all but decided that I'd never have children, especially not a son. It choked me to imagine raising a child and then watching him join a gang, wind up behind bars, die inside. How did all these luckless Chicago women endure it?

Yep, the funeral home was nearly full. Certainly a better turnout than the annual reunion of the Lisles, where all the mayhem seemed to begin. Frail, gentle old Clay Jackson had asked Hero to contact Woody about the disappearance of his granddaughter Lavelle. A simple enough request, but look what it had led to: Hero dead, Ivy's guts shot out, and me no longer a virgin.

Woody was much more torn up than I would have predicted. He cried and cried into his big white hanky. Maybe his tears weren't only for his nephew. Maybe he was crying about Ivy, too. It can't have been far from his mind that we might all be gathered here again in the near future, weeping for her.

There was to be no burial. Hero would be cremated.

As the mourners were filing out at the end of the viewing, I caught sight of June Barker. She was looking in our direction, but when I made eye contact she looked away and picked up her pace.

June had been unfriendly the day that Ivy and I dropped in at her place. Sure, a ladies club type like Ivy wasn't good for the whorehouse business; but that wasn't the only reason June had wanted us out of there. I had the feeling then that she knew more than she was telling us. If anything, she'd be twice as uncooperative now that the stakes had been kicked up. It was no longer just a matter of Lavelle disappearing. Bodies were piling up. After Ivy was shot, Jack Klaus had pulled in a number of Forest Street residents for questioning, including June, but he got nothing out of her.

I was willing to risk June's ire, figuring she wouldn't jump too nasty with me at a family funeral. But by the time I got through the clumps of people blocking my path, she was long gone. I saw the mourners surrounding my great-uncle and figured he might need rescuing. I fought my way back to his side.

Woody would rather die than have a minister at Hero's funeral. I figured a lot of the attendees felt cheated out of a sermon. No opportunity to weep and wail. But maybe some free booze and homemade grub would make up for being robbed of that outlet. One of Woody's cousins was hosting a reception at her home out in Altgeld Gardens. That was a low-rise/low-rent development on the edge of the city, a subsidized city-housing experiment that had gone wrong and ultimately morphed into a nightmare on a par with the Robert Taylor Homes.

At any rate, Woody and I begged off. We wanted to get over to the hospital to check on Ivy.

* * *

She was the color of a saltine, but she was alive. Alive and barely awake, just enough to show her awareness and dismay over all the tubes and wires and monitors. She was doing a weird, enervated pantomime with her round-the-clock nurse.

"Thirsty," the woman explained to us.

I fed her ice chips while Woody held her poor hand and stared into her eyes. His face was oily with tears. No wonder. I'd never seen anybody look like that, nobody living, I mean.

So many things I wanted to say to her. I mumbled a prayer that I'd get the chance to say them. I wanted to talk to her about me and Melvin. If things were normal she might not even need to be told. Eagle-eyed Ivy might just have sensed that change in my life. I wanted to talk to her about Hero, not his death, which of course we were keeping from her, but his life. He was another part of that haze hanging over my early days. And I wanted her to tell me about my mother, answer those questions she had been deflecting for the last ten years.

She tried to stay awake and visit with us, but she wasn't up to the effort. Just before she went under again, she grunted at the nurse, who nodded at her. "Yes, ma'am, I'm gonna tell them. You rest now."

"Tell who?" I asked. "What did that mean?"

"Mrs. Lisle got herself in a real state this morning. I'm

not too sure I know what she said or what it means. She wanted me to let you know something about some clay. I could barely understand her. But she said I must tell you there was clay on the gun at home, or maybe the gun was lost in the clay. Or something like that."

Woody understood immediately. So did I. Ivy was telling us Clay Jackson had something to do with the shooting.

Before I could even speak, Woody was rushing out of the door.

"Just a minute, for christsake!"

I'd never spoken to Woody that way before.

"Just hold on for a minute," I begged. "What that nurse said was all garbled. Maybe she heard wrong. Or Ivy could have been delirious. We can't just storm into his house and lynch him."

That seemed to penetrate. The blood in my uncle's eyes receded.

"Besides," I said, "remember what Jack Klaus told you. The police figure one of the two guys who jumped us was probably the shooter. It makes sense, doesn't it? These idiots who keep coming at us—the guy who beat me up under the IC tracks, the one who killed Hero, the one who shot Ivy— they've all got to be tied in with each other somehow. But surely not with Clay Jackson?"

"You're right, Cass. But I'm going to find out what all that garbled stuff meant. One way or another. And if Clay did have anything to do with what happened, God help him."

He appeared to be heeding my words of caution, but as soon as we reached Clay Jackson's apartment building he turned into the hanging judge again. Woody was stomping up the stairs so hard the building seemed to vibrate.

Mr. Jackson answered the door in his bathrobe. I guess the old man had been napping. He shrank away from Woody, who was booming at him: "What do you know about a gun, Clay? What the hell did you do?"

Jackson began to stutter out his confused answer standing there at the door, but Woody shoved him back inside.

"Go ahead, man. What's this about a gun? You know who shot my wife?"

"No, no, Mr. Woody. Miss Ivy found it and then she left out of here. I don't know who hurt her."

"Goddammit, man. What are you talking about?"

Jackson scooted over to a sagging chest of drawers. He lifted the gun out and handed it to Woody, butt first.

"Miss Ivy found it in Lavelle's room. She tole me let's her and me go over everything we can find in there and this was up in a closet, taped over the door sill."

Woody held the .45 as though at any moment he might

use it to smash something to bits. Clay was scared. Even I took a few steps away from my uncle.

"You never saw it before, Mr. Jackson?" I asked.

"Naw. Never."

"And you have no idea who shot at Ivy after she left here?"

"I swear I don't. I don't know how y'all could even believe something like that. After you was helping me with Lavelle, and after everything Miss Ivy done for me all these years. I wouldn't be no kind of a man to turn on y'all that way."

"We know, Mr. Jackson, we know. I'm very sorry if you thought we were accusing you. Why don't you show me Lavelle's room."

We left Woody in the front room holding that gun and looking about as lethal as it did.

It looked as though Clay and Ivy had done a pretty thorough job of searching. The room was inside out. But I made a cursory tour, anyway. I lifted the covers and checked beneath the bed, I opened the drawers of her bureau, flipped through a couple of paperbacks on a shelf. There was a dressing table littered with the expected things: hair oil, lipsticks, mismatched earrings in a little bowl. I picked up a ragged-tooth Afro pick. And for some reason I didn't put it right back in its place. I didn't know why, but I held onto it, almost the way Woody was cradling that gun.

Clay was standing across the room watching me. I didn't blame him for remaining with me rather than going back to face Woody's wrath.

"Mr. Jackson, you remember telling us about Lavelle's friend Luther, don't you?"

"Yes."

"But you never met him, right? You don't know what he looks like."

"Naw, I don't."

"I met him," I said, "and he doesn't have a natural. His hair's got that gunky stuff in it. A process."

"If that's what you say."

I went back into the other room.

"Woody."

He looked up.

"We should go now."

"What?"

"We should thank Mr. Jackson and go now."

He clearly didn't know why I said that, but he followed my lead anyway. As soon as we were on the stairs again, I told him, "That guy at the hardware store—what did he say about Luther?"

"What are you talking about, Cass? You saying that dog Luther's behind the shooting?"

"No. I asked Garrick—or maybe you did—if he dealt directly with Lavelle or if he went through her pimp, Luther."

"Yes, I remember that."

"And he said he never had any truck with that Afro-head nigger, or something like that."

"Yes."

"You understand now? What did Luther's hair look like?"

"Fried. All straightened out. He doesn't wear an Afro."

"That's right. So Garrick was talking about some other man in Lavelle's life. Maybe another pimp. We need to see Garrick again. And if he won't talk to us—"

"Jack Klaus could make him. Let's go."

The storefront looked much as it had the last time. But now there was no answer to Woody's rapping at the front door, and inside the shop there was no sign of life. In one of the walk-up apartments above the store, the volume suddenly went way up on a radio. Somebody was grooving to "Chain of Fools."

We walked to the end of the block and then took the alley to the back of the hardware store. The rusty aluminum gate was padlocked.

"What now?" I asked.

He could only shake his head and cuss quietly.

"Is it a coincidence he's not here? Or is he gone for good?"

Woody kicked at the gate. Once and then again, even stronger. Then he stooped and picked up an empty Vienna sausage tin. He threw it with all his might at the back entrance to Garrick's place. When that didn't do the trick for him, he picked up a stone and threw that. Then a chunk of brick. Any debris he could get his hands on he hurled at the door. He was pouring sweat and looking crazy. I waited until the fury passed.

In a minute he stopped his frenzied acting out. We stood in the alley, broken glass twinkling all around us like some kind of junkyard fairyland. It stank back there. A terrible-looking dog stalked past us.

"Mighta been better if niggers had burned it all to the ground," Woody said. "Everywhere in the world. Start all over. Clean."

"I know."

"I don't know if you do, sugar. Maybe you too young to feel that way."

"No. Not really."

"That's right. You're one of these serious young ones. Always were."

"I think 'depressed' is more like it."

He let the stick he was holding drop to the dirt. "All right, Cass. We won't accomplish a damn thing standing here feeling sorry. We'll stop in at the hospital first, and then I'm calling Klaus. It's time to get back to basics. One way or another that'll get us who shot Ivy. And that nigger will be mine."

"What basics do you mean?"

"Lavelle Jackson. She's basic. And a high school ring. A dead white gal. And a luckless nigger boy named Eddie Quick."

FIFTEEN

Jack Klaus had a home out on Archer Avenue. Territory so foreign to me, I thought we'd left the city limits. One grotesquely shingled house after another. It was a gray, gray place and the quietness of the streets was more menacing than restful. I'd rather be dead than living in a place like it. But obviously not everybody felt the same. During the fair-housing marches in neighborhoods like this one, the residents had thrown rotten vegetables at Dr. King and spat on the nuns walking arm in arm with him.

The lawns were sprouting green and the streets were clean, and the price of cornflakes and laundry detergent, posted on the supermarket windows, seemed to be about half what they were getting for those items in Black Metropolis.

There was another reason I was paying such close attention to our surroundings: growing apprehension, or call it paranoia, that some white thugs might spot us and start to follow the car. Woody may have felt it, too. I didn't know and I didn't mention it. Horrible fear and anger began to rise in me, and Ivy's old trick of counting to ten wasn't working. The only way I had to push my feelings down was to think how terrified I'd be if we were in Mississippi or Alabama. They have it worse, I kept telling myself. Compared to them, you're lucky.

Woody parked in the rear driveway. Klaus was waiting for us at the back door. He led us not into the house but directly into a finished garage which had been turned into a family room replete with fake wood paneling and Ping-Pong setup.

He had laid out a card table with hot coffee and sandwiches and store-bought pound cake.

"I thought you and Cass might be hungry."

I snapped to. That was overly familiar, his calling me Cass. I didn't like it.

"Thank you kindly," Woody said, pouring himself coffee.

"How is she, Woody?"

"My lady will pull through. She's going to make it."

"I hope you give her my good wishes."

"Will do. You been able to pick up on Carl Garrick, the hardware store man?"

"No. His wife says he left home for work a couple of days ago, like always, and never came back. He called her once to say he's all right, but wouldn't tell her where he was. You and Cassandra are right. Garrick knows something."

"How's your family, Jack?"

"We're fine. Laura's got the kids at her mom's place. They ought to be home soon. That's why I thought we better do this out here. It's private."

What's private? I thought.

But then I looked over at the Ping-Pong table. It was covered with papers: typewritten sheets, forms, handwritten notes, folders, photographs. These last were what caught my attention. A series of police mug shots showed the face of the burly man my uncle Hero had killed. The same man who had snatched my bag and mauled me under the IC tracks. The name REGGIE GREEN was printed at the bottom of each photo. Charges against him ran the gamut from extortion to armed robbery to rape to attempted homicide. So I had almost been raped by a career criminal named Reggie, a name I had always disliked. I'd never met a Reggie I trusted. Black women really should stop naming their sons that.

Neither Woody nor I had been able to give much of a description of the second man, the one who killed Uncle Hero. He was medium brown, medium height, and it had all happened in the dark. Klaus told us the police were checking out ex-cons known to have done time with Reggie Green.

I scanned the other pages. One of the manila folders held the photocopied paperwork on the Eddie Lee Quick case. I picked it up.

Woody was showing Klaus the gun from Clay Jackson's apartment. While they talked, I read quickly.

On October 18, 1959, two men found the raped and slaughtered body of Liz Greevy, who taught Special Education at the Champlain Elementary School. Those men were janitor Tom Springer and science teacher Wally Humphrey. Humphrey summoned the patrolman walking his beat near the school yard.

The patrolman was one Charles Ryan, who in turn notified the homicide squad at the precinct house. The two detectives who caught the call and subsequently worked the case were Sergeant Zeke Shelton and Detective Anthony Carmen. All parties, including the victim, were white.

Eddie Lee Quick, a fourteen-year-old Negro variously described as being "slow witted," "an outsized adolescent," and "an ox," was found hiding in the boiler room and arrested the same afternoon as the murder.

Other notes, reports, and newspaper clippings listed prominent attorney Jerome Kapperstein, well known for his involvement with civil rights causes, as counsel for the defense.

I took particular notice of one paragraph in the newspaper coverage of the trial. The prosecutor, it said, wanted to impose a life sentence, but due to recent changes in the law, that was no longer allowed. The jury handed down a sentence of seventy-five years.

Woody took the folder from my hands and did his own quick reading of the papers inside. Meanwhile, I opened another folder. This one was marked ZEKE SHELTON. It too contained a mug shot.

"I don't understand," I said. "Wasn't he the lead detective in the case?"

"That's right," Klaus said. "They say Shelton was a hell of a cop once. But that hasn't been true for a long time. He's the worst kind of scum."

"Why?"

"Because he runs interference for South Side drug and policy operations. He's in Henry Waddell's pocket for sure."

"That soulless nigger's got a hand in more evil than a Dixie senator," Woody growled. "They oughta hang him by his goddamn neck."

I was startled to hear my uncle use that language in front of a white man. I felt my face go red, in fact. But I said nothing. I kept reading.

Klaus told me, "It looked as though Internal Affairs had nailed Zeke Shelton a few years back. He was convicted and on the way to Joliet. But he had a judge in his pocket, or Waddell did. The verdict was overturned."

"And he's the one who put Eddie Quick away?"

"Yeah. He threw himself into his work, too. I always thought something stunk about the way they hustled that kid into prison."

"Had you also heard Eddie Quick was beaten into confessing?" I asked.

"I heard maybe that happened. Yeah."

"Was it Shelton who did the beating?"

"No way to know which one of the cops at the station house did that. But I'd bet Shelton got in his licks."

"Is he still on the force?"

"Yeah."

"He doesn't know you're helping us? With Lavelle Jackson or anything else."

"No. And I've got to keep it that way. Woody understands that. I hope you do, too."

"Of course I do. What do you think I am, a moron?"

Maybe I shouldn't have gone after him that way; maybe he wasn't patronizing me. I wasn't sure. I just knew something about him annoyed me.

Woody put down the notes. "Far as I see it, only four people could have taken that ring off the teacher's body—the two civilians who discovered the body; the first cop on the scene, Ryan; or Eddie Lee Quick himself. But the ring was never found in Quick's possession. Fact, from the morning of the day she was killed, nobody had seen the ring until Lavelle Jackson left it in the grocery store."

"It's for damn sure Quick didn't have it with him in the slam all this time," Klaus added.

He pressed food on us but we declined. Then I relented and took a slice of the cake. Sara Lee, I concluded.

"By the way," Woody said, "anything come up on either of the other cops? Shelton's partner, Tony Carmen, or Ryan, the beat cop?"

"No. Carmen is dead. If he was dirty, too, we don't know about it. And as for Charlie Ryan, he's straight arrow. He rides a desk these days."

"What about the two school guys?" I asked.

"The science teacher and the maintenance man? No, nothing."

Klaus and Woody went over a few other details and I went back to the newspaper coverage of the sensational murder and the ensuing trial. Funny, whoever compiled the newspaper stories had neglected to include clippings from the black press. I recalled Woody and Ivy telling me how the *Banner* had tried to dig into the Eddie Lee Quick case. I also remember their speculation that the reporters were frightened or bought off.

We left Lavelle's .45 with Jack Klaus, who said he'd start

a trace on it as soon as he got to work the next day. "Don't get your hopes up, though," he warned us. "This could've come from anywhere."

As Woody was backing out of the driveway, another car suddenly turned in. We missed a smashup by a hair. For a half minute or so, all parties sat unmoving, recovering our breath. The only sound to be heard was an almost subliminal music. At the wheel of the other vehicle was a rather pretty woman in her late thirties. Two children on the backseat. No doubt they were Klaus's wife and kids. On their car radio, the Fifth Dimension was singing "Up, Up and Away."

SIXTEEN

The morning was glorious, made all the better by Ivy's improved condition. Woody and I had a quick breakfast at home, bought as many flowers as our arms could hold, and then spent most of the morning at her bedside. We left her dozing under the gaze of the hired nurse.

Outside, the strong, sweet air had blown away the last of the smoke hanging over the city. I was behind the wheel of Ivy's coupe. It felt just as great as I thought it would. But unfortunately I wasn't sporting Bobby around, which was always part of the fantasy. I wasn't on the way to a pleasant afternoon at the Morton Arboretum or bombing along Lake

Shore Drive with the radio on ultra rock. Instead I was back in the old neighborhood, and if things went as I figured they would, June Barker would soon be looking me up and down with that hateful snarl on her lips.

One thing was different, of course. Woody. Not too likely she'd pull that sullen act on him. He must have been a tough bastard in his youth. One generation after another, neighborhood people feared him and knew enough not to cross him. He was quick with that razor of his now. I could just imagine how he must have handled it in his youth.

We were kept waiting a long while at the front door but finally someone answered. Not June. It was a young woman I'd never seen before. June was out, she told us.

Until when? we pressed.

"Until she gits back."

Slam.

I drove away while she watched us from behind the curtains, but then I circled back and parked across the street several houses down from the Barker place. Within twenty minutes a livery cab pulled up at the door and June came out of the house. The car turned onto Vincennes and I followed.

I followed it back to the fringes of my own neighborhood. There was an invisible color line in Hyde Park. More than one, actually. No U of C students crossed it except for the occasional foray to a barbecue joint or a blues club. June got out at the corner of Fiftieth and Ellis and walked a few doors north to an apartment building. We watched as she rang one of the doorbells, fidgeted, and then rang again and again.

After five minutes or so, a tall man with nappy, graying hair appeared from the rear of the building. He was toting garbage. June spoke briefly to him, then she turned and left. I trailed her to the bus stop on Garfield Boulevard, and when the bus arrived she got on.

We headed back to the building on Ellis. Woody got out and greeted the maintenance man politely. I watched from the car.

"What did he say?" I asked when he returned.

"June was looking for a gal who lives here. Name of Antonia Riddle."

"You think this is a branch of the Forest Street whorehouse?"

"I don't know. Says this Tonia has men friends coming around pretty regular. But there's no commotion in her place. She's a decent young woman. Pays her rent. Far as he knows, she's putting herself through school. Just like you are."

* * *

You'd think—for somebody as self-absorbed as I am, some-body who has spent as much time as I have wallowing in old hurts, poking at memories, playing at being my own analyst—you'd think a relic from times past wouldn't hold any more power over me.

Oh how wrong you'd be.

The sight of Champlain Elementary School made me ill. In about two seconds one of those scenes from my wretched school days was playing in my head. Snow piled up against the buildings. Children in puffy coats with hoods and wet mittens. It is lunchtime and the boys are throwing snowballs into which they've packed rocks or shards of glass. As I cross the school yard one of them gets me in the face. The boy who threw it is laughing and calling me one of a half dozen names he has for me. He is among the most feared boys at the school. I call him a retard, which infuriates him. He runs toward me in a rage, but he slips on the ice at my feet. The world seems to go red somehow. I cannot account for what I do. First I kick him in the head. Then, as he tries to rise, I kick him in the ribs. I pick up a huge stone, fall to my knees, and begin to pound his face with it. I don't remember how it ended. I only recall how angry my grandmother was at having to come to the school later in the week. And I recall the boy's mother telling her I should be put in a mental hospital.

It was sort of like being under water, walking those halls. I was holding my breath, the way you do under water.

The principal in my day was a pinched, sadistic old thing, Mrs. DeHaan. Rimless spectacles. Lace-up orthopaedic shoes. White muslin stockings. A brooch she wore every fucking day: it was a watch face with a ballpoint pen attached by a thin gold chain.

Extremely convenient how the Board of Ed's decision to install black principals in black schools dovetailed so nicely with white teachers fearing for their lives in black neighborhoods. No more Mrs. DeHaans. In some quarters they called that progress, which always comes at a price.

The current principal, Lucille Crooks, was black and bosomy in a burnt orange linen frock. She stood and greeted Woody as if she'd met him before. When the pleasantries were over, she was not glad to learn why we were visiting.

"I don't know if I can accommodate you, Mr. Lisle. Why are you curious about our records?"

"I'm hoping to be of some help to an old friend whose granddaughter went to school here at Champlain. Her name is Lavelle Jackson. She's missing."

"I see. I can't allow you to read the file, but I'll take a look."

Mrs. Crooks went to the door and we heard her repeat the name to one of the secretaries.

"Thank you for your efforts, but it's not just Lavelle's records I'm interested in."

"Oh? What else did you want?"

"Employment records."

"My teachers, you mean?"

"Yes. Teachers and staff."

"That could cause all kinds of problems, Mr. Lisle. I couldn't possibly . . ."

"Maybe I can narrow it down for you. I want to see the records on a teacher who was working here at the time of the Elizabeth Greevy murder. Wallace Humphrey. And I want to look at any paperwork you have on a Tom Springer, a maintenance man."

The principal had gone rigid in her leather chair. "I won't have this, Mr. Lisle."

"Won't have what?"

"I will not have this school dragged into the spotlight again. That was before my time, all of that mess. You have something to do with that boy who murdered a teacher here. You're working with his family to get him released from prison."

"No, you have it wrong," he said sharply. "Look, I was hoping you could help us out without me going into too many details. I'm just going to ask you if you heard about a shooting out here a few days ago."

"I did. Something happened on Forest Street."

"I guess you don't know the woman shot was my wife."

"You mean Mrs. Lisle was . . ."

"Yes, that's right, Mrs. Lisle. And I'm not about to leave this thing alone until I know who did it."

She sat speechless as one of the assistants walked in and placed a folder on her desk. After the woman had gone, she opened her desk drawer and took out a Kleenex and proceeded to blot the moisture on her forehead and neck.

"What does Mrs. Lisle's attack have to do with this school? Or this Lavelle Johnson?"

"Jackson," I said.

"Jackson. You say you're not trying to reopen the murder case. Then what are you after, you and your niece?"

I answered. "We can't spell that out in twenty-five words, Mrs. Crooks. Right now we don't know how many words it's going to take. But the murder of that teacher and the shooting of my great-aunt and the disappearance of Lavelle Jackson are all part of the same—well, at least the same paragraph."

She was looking at me funny. "You attended school here, you said?"

"For a while."

I suppose she was weighing all the factors, letting things sink in. A minute later she asked if we'd mind waiting outside the office for a few moments.

When she called us back in she told us that Tom Springer was being summoned.

"Wally Humphrey retired a year and a half ago," she announced. "He has a heart condition. He's quite an elderly man."

"It would help if you gave me his number at home," Woody said.

"I don't know it, Mr. Lisle. Mr. Humphrey went to live with his grandchildren in Maine."

Tom Springer's dull blue eyes almost matched the uniform he wore. Except for his startled expression when he noticed Woody in the room, he did not look directly at any of us. Rather, he had a way of lowering his head so that his forehead was almost parallel to the floor, and then rolling his eyes up when someone talked to him.

Maybe he thought he had a James Dean thing working. At any rate, he wasn't what I was expecting. You expect the school janitor to be on the chubby side, bald, and either very sweet tempered or very disagreeable. If I hadn't read about him in the file Jack Klaus had compiled for us I'd have expected a black man rather than a white one.

Springer was of slender build, maybe forty-five, with a full head of faded blond hair. Woody wished him good afternoon. But instead of doing the same he asked, "What is it now?"

We looked at him blankly.

"Come on. No need to play dumb. She's been ratting on me again, right?"

I didn't know what the hell he was talking about, but I predicted trouble. It startled me when he went on to make a joke.

"I thought for sure," he said, "old Blubber Butt was bad-mouthing me again to my union. I expected to see a rep sitting in here. By the way, I hope you ain't her husband."

The aforesaid Blubber Butt was no doubt Mrs. Crooks, who had stepped out for a few moments while we talked.

"No," said Woody. "I'm not Mrs. Crooks's husband. And as far as I know, your job is safe."

Springer grinned and lit a cigarette. "Okay. So what's the deal?"

"My name's Woody Lisle. This is my grand-niece, Cassandra."

He nodded. "Okay. So what's the deal?"

"Bear with me, Mr. Springer. I'll get to the deal in a minute."

He gave Woody another roll of his eyes. "Where you from, Lisle?"

"Spent time in Louisiana as a young man. But I'm a Chicagoan. Why do you ask?"

"You don't sound like most of them—I mean, you talk pretty well. What are you? A new teacher?"

"No."

"You from the Board of Ed, then? Got yourself one of them good cushy jobs they're handing out down there, huh?"

"That's right."

"I didn't care much for education myself," Springer said. "You know—bored of education. Get it?"

"Mr. Springer, you've worked at the school for quite a few years now, haven't you?"

"Right."

"Know the neighborhood pretty well?"

"You bet."

"I wonder if you know Pleasant's Grocery, over on Forty-third?"

"Yeah. There's a colored fella named Shep runs it."

"What about the children here at the school? You like kids? Or do they kind of get on your nerves?"

"They don't bother me, I don't bother them."

"You a married man, Mr. Springer? Children of your own?"

"Nah. Natural-born bachelor, that's me."

"What about parents of the kids? Do you know any of them by name?"

He shrugged. "Not really. I see the mamas come in when

one of 'em gets suspended or something. Sometimes Blubber Butt will haul one of 'em in here about something the kid's done."

"Do you know a neighborhood resident called Clay Jackson?"

"Doesn't ring a bell. He got kids here?"

"No. Actually he's an older man. His granddaughter attended this school years ago. Lavelle Jackson."

"Half the kids in here got a name like Jackson. But I don't know those two people. Fact is, I put in my hours and go home. My friends don't live in this part of town. Know what I mean? No offense, though. You understand what I'm saying."

"I do. I do, Mr. Springer."

"That about wrap it up?"

"Almost. Just a few more questions if you can spare the time."

"You writing a book or something—about janitors and how exciting our lives are?"

"Close. Actually I'm writing about old crimes. Crimes that took place on school property."

"Crimes?"

"Yes."

The blue eyes rolled my way for an instant. "Oh, brother. I shoulda known."

That kicked off an odd association. There was a Negro

actor who specialized in shuffling, servile roles. His name was Willie Best. My grandmother had been a devotee of a TV sitcom called *The Stu Erwin Show*, where Best had played the idiotic family servant.

The white man in the room with us, Tom Springer, wasn't kowtowing to Woody and me, and I sensed he knew we weren't really from the school board. But his manner did smack of the village idiot.

"I understand you were right on the spot when Liz Greevy was murdered here. I figured I'd have to go a long way to find another witness as good as you. You're quoted in all the newspapers from that time."

"I don't know about being a witness. I just came up on her in the book room, all cut up like that. Mr. Humphrey and me. We both found her."

"I know it's asking a lot of you. But do you remember why you went to the book room?"

"We was looking all over for her. We searched the whole building before we found her."

"And why were you looking for her?"

" 'Cause nobody'd seen her since lunchtime. Knew something musta happened to her."

"I see. Were you and Mr. Humphrey together when you found the body? Or did one of you find her and then yell out to the other one?"

"We found her at the same time."

"All right. That must have been a horrible sight, the young teacher all cut up, all that blood."

"Yeah. I never saw anything so bad." He lifted his shoulders and made a charade of shivering with fright.

The village idiot. Was that really it? Or was the dumbness a put-on? The thing about Springer was that he seemed to know how lame his answers were, but he didn't much care.

"Did you happen to notice if Liz Greevy was wearing a ring?"

"What?"

"A ring. With a fairly large stone. A high school ring."

"Oh, that. No. I couldn't get out of there fast enough. I didn't notice no ring."

"Right. You ran out and called a policeman who was nearby."

"Yes—I mean no. Mr. Humphrey went and got him."

"And you? Where did you run to?"

"Probably back to my room, back near the boiler."

"And you waited there until all the detectives arrived?"

"Yeah, I guess so."

"You ran back there because you were scared, is that it?"

"Um hum. I was real scared."

"I see. What kind of person was Mr. Humphrey anyway? A good man, would you say?"

"I guess he was okay. How should I know? People around here don't have no damn use for me unless they're screaming about the heat or the mice in the lunchroom."

"Teachers don't pay much attention to you, is that it? Sometimes act like maybe they're above you? Better than you?"

He shrugged.

"Do you remember the boy who did the killing?"

"Eddie."

"Right. Ever speak to him?"

"No. I told you, I don't bother nobody."

"Yes, I heard you. It's just that Eddie Quick wasn't an ordinary student. Didn't you ever notice how big he was? Did you ever see him and think he looked older than most of the other children?"

"He was a retard. I didn't pay much mind."

"Apparently Miss Greevy was fond of Eddie, though. I think I read somewhere that she'd taken him under her wing, let him run little errands for her, and so on."

"I wouldn't know."

"Did you see Eddie when the detectives found him down there in the boiler room?"

"Yeah. He was crying and all."

"He must've been covered in blood, right?"

"I guess so. I mean, he'd have to be, right?"

"I don't know, Mr. Springer. Was he?"

"Yeah, I think he was. But they carried him out real fast. So I didn't see that."

"Well, thank you very much." Woody turned to me then. "I think we have enough research for that chapter, don't you, Cass?"

"Yes."

"I'll let you get back to work now, Mr. Springer."

"You be sure and send me a copy of that book. What was your name again?"

SEVENTEEN

"What do you think?" I asked as we walked through the school parking lot.

Woody threw the question back at me. "What do you think?"

"Something's not right about that guy. He's hiding something and doesn't give a damn whether we know it or not. He's having fun playing the dummy. Kind of his way of saying 'screw you.' "

"That's what I think. It's like he figures nobody can touch him. Insolent redneck."

"Do you think he killed Liz Greevy?"

"Maybe."

"Even if he didn't, do you believe Eddie Lee Quick was innocent?"

"I'm a ways from being sure about that."

So was I. But that didn't prevent me from making the leap in my mind. What if that boy's only crime was being black and slow?

It was easy to pity Eddie Lee Quick. I was undergoing that empathy that I always felt reading an engrossing novel. Feeling a character's pain, allowing the full brunt of what was happening on the page to seep into my heart. Just as quickly as I'd latched on to Eddie Quick's pain, I let go of it, however. Something else was knocking around in my mind now, knocking hard.

"Hold it a minute," I said.

"Did you forget something?"

I must have looked like a real moron. Standing still, blinking. I was trying to catch the tail of a thought before it got away from me. All at once I had it.

"Woody. Oh, Lord, Woody."

"What?"

"We have to go back to that building on Ellis. Where June was trying to see the girl called Antonia Riddle."

"What for?"

"You have to find that maintenance man again. You've gotta ask him where Antonia Riddle goes to school. Ask if she goes to Debs."

"Why?"

I looked at him blankly, trying to decide whom to answer first—him or the voice in my head. *It can't possibly be true.* That's what I was telling myself. *But then again, it almost has to be.*

When Woody told me the name of the girl who lived in that building, it was as if a little piston began firing somewhere in my brain. Now I knew what that was about. The super in the building said Tonia was a decent young lady, or something like that. *Tonia*, short for Antonia. *Putting herself through school—just like you.* At the end of that first encounter with Melvin in the Root office, a girl he called Tanya had made fun of me. I could hear him now, saying "What's happening, Tanya?"

But he hadn't really said "Tanya." He called her *Tonia*.

I'd made a flippant remark about Antonia Riddle's place being a branch of the Forest Street brothel. Suddenly that wasn't so funny. Maybe yesterday I wouldn't have been so ready to see all the connections. But now, with all the threads of Lavelle Jackson's disappearance tying in with the Eddie Lee Quick case, it was starting to look like everything and everyone I'd seen and heard over the last week were of a piece.

We made the trip back to the Ellis Street apartment building. Woody located the maintenance man, slipped him a twenty. The man consulted two of the neighbors. It was soon confirmed. Antonia Riddle, lanky and light skinned, was a student at Debs College.

I told Woody I needed a little time to make a play that might get us some answers. Just follow along, I said.

I also continued to play chauffeur. Next to me on the front seat Woody smoked one of his big cigars. I didn't break in on his thoughts and he didn't interrupt mine.

Eddie Quick was linked to Liz Greevy. Liz Greevy was linked to Lavelle Jackson. Lavelle linked to June, to Garrick, to Luther, and to the yet-to-be-identified "Afro." June linked to Luther, probably to Afro, and to Tonia. Tonia linked to Root, meaning Melvin and Bobby. Where did it end? Where did the shotgun blasts that almost took Ivy's life fit in? And me, was I part of the chain, too? Where did I fit?

"Watch where you're going, Cass," Woody warned me. "You're too close to that car up ahead."

"Sorry."

"Where in hell are you driving us, anyway?"

"Well, you just got out of elementary school. But you're smart enough to skip high school altogether. Don't you think it's time you went to college?"

I could picture Woody walking confidently into a United Nations' session. I could easily imagine him wrestling a tiger, playing the flute, delivering a baby, flying a plane. But when we walked into the lobby of Debs College, he became strangely shy, following rather than leading. He didn't talk much, either.

I had it in mind to track down Owen and introduce him to Woody. But at the last moment I decided against it. A sudden prick of instinct told me it might not be appropriate to bring those two together. A privileged white Southerner, sweet and sympathetic as he was, and an older black man whose family had survived the murderous centuries down there. Some knot of misery, guilt, or hatred, long buried like a hot stone in the belly, might suddenly explode. No. That dialectic, as my history professor was so fond of saying, would have to wait.

I jiggled the doorknob on the Root office door. Locked, as usual. I knocked, too. But there was no answer. Then I pressed my ear against the glass that was perpetually covered with impenetrable construction paper. It wasn't that I heard a sound; what I heard was a particular kind of soundlessness. What is it that makes you think there's a living presence on the other side of a door? Of course you can't pin that down; it's just one of those things you sense.

While I carried on the search for Melvin, I gave Woody a tour of the premises. Every few minutes I'd circle back to the Root office, trying to nab anybody coming or going.

I got into the registrar's office just as they were closing for the day. The secretary looked up Tonia Riddle's schedule for me.

"She has an evening class. It meets tonight at eight."

It was time for something to eat; moreover, something to drink. That meant the Yacht Club. If Woody hadn't suggested it, I would have.

The bar was in full swing. I looked quickly at the two stools Bobby and I had occupied on so many occasions. Somehow I knew we'd never sit there again, laughing, bitching about this or that. We'd never tease each other again. It hurt me like a burn.

We found a booth at the back and ordered drinks.

"What's good here?" Woody asked me as he looked over the hand-printed menu.

"Beer."

He laughed. "Besides that, Daisy Mae."

"Pizza."

"Is that all?"

"The spaghetti's okay. Good garlic bread."

"All right. Let's have that."

Woody excused himself and went to use the coin phone near the toilets. He was checking on Ivy and also phoning Jack Klaus to see if anything had developed from his end.

I got out my cigarettes, tasted some of the creamy ale,

my mind wandering. What song was playing that day when Bobby and I were crying about Martin's assassination? Something by Billie Holiday, maybe? No. James Brown?

Somebody in the place tonight had a thing for Buffalo Springfield. The jukebox played one after another of their songs. But then Otis Redding replaced them. Next were battling versions of "Heard It Through the Grapevine": first Marvin's and then Gladys Knight's.

Just as the Supremes' greatest hits got started, I caught a glimpse of a stellar presence on the campus—Danny Helm, the SDS leader. We were both in Professor Bluestein's labor history class, but Danny had stopped coming to class weeks before I did. He sure was intense, I had to give that to him. And smart. I'd heard him speak at the teach-in. He was also tall, with a mop of chestnut curls and limpid brown eyes, and about a million white girls wanted to go to bed with him.

Woody's jaw looked tight when he came back to the table.

"Is she worse?"

"No, baby. She's doing pretty fair. She even tried to say a few words to me."

"That's great."

He nodded.

"So why are you angry?"

"I haven't got him yet, that's why. I already told you, Cass, when I find out who did this to Ivy, I'll have to kill him."

"Yes, sir, I know." And I did. I wanted him dead, too. With all the hate I had in me, of course I did. And I wanted his death to take a long time.

Still, I had to hope Woody's words were just male braggadocio. Spending his final years of life behind bars was not one of the many things I imagined he could do. The second guy from that night Woody and I were jumped—the one who got away—if he shot Ivy, I wanted the cops to find him before Woody did.

We ate our meal in relative silence. If I hadn't decided afterward to have a cup of coffee we might have missed Melvin. He was walking toward the men's room when I spotted him.

I called out his name.

He whirled around, looking hunted. Close to the same reaction he'd had that day in the cafeteria. He didn't like to be surprised and he didn't like to be noticed. But when he realized it was me, his expression softened a bit. As he walked over to our table, however, his eyes switched to Woody.

"Melvin," I said, "I need to know something."

He didn't ask what I wanted to know. He was still staring at Woody.

"This is my—this is Woody Lisle. He raised me."

"Lisle," he repeated. "Yeah, I thought that was you. I didn't realize when Cassandra mentioned you that you were the same one who used to do dirty Uncle Tom shit for the city machine. Ain't that right? You used to be one of Daley's house niggas."

Woody didn't even blink. He asked, "This one of your little friends, Cass?"

"Melvin, don't talk to him that way," I said.

Woody placed a hand on my arm. "Never mind, honey. Would you like to join us, Mr. . . . ?"

"No. Hell, no."

"You're being a rude asshole, Melvin." And with that remark, I realized something: I'd had sex, the first of my life, with a man whose last name I didn't know. I'd have laughed if I weren't so sure that with Melvin's next insult, Woody was going to try to knock him down.

"Did you hear what I said, Melvin? I need to ask you something."

"What is it now? If it's about Bobby, forget it. Just forget him, period."

"What do you mean, 'forget him'?"

He didn't answer.

"You have real kindness in you," I said. "I know you do. Can't you see I'm worried about him?"

"Be cool. Nothing much gone happen to him, girl. Just some reeducation."

I see. We think we're in China now.

I had to fight myself to keep from saying it. "There was a girl in your office the other day. Tonia."

"Yeah?"

"Is her last name Riddle? Does she live in Kenwood?"

"Why?"

"Jesus, why can't you answer a simple question? Don't you trust anyone?"

He laughed. Nasty, knowing. The way Tonia Riddle had laughed at me.

"I'll take that as a 'yes,' Melvin. You listen to me now."

"Fuck you. Oops. I already did."

"Woody, don't!" I tackled him as he rose to start punching. "Melvin, listen to me . . ."

"No, he better listen to me," Woody said and turned on him. "What do you know about the shooting of a woman on Forest Street, you animal?"

"What street? I got no idea what you talking about. You better sit down, old man." He began to walk away, not toward the toilet in the rear, but toward the entrance to the bar.

"Wait a minute, Melvin—please," I called.

"Later for you. Y'all are both crazy. I got business to do."

"You're not going to die gloriously, Melvin."

"I'll do better than you."

"Goddammit," I yelled after him, "you better tell Tonia she's playing with fire."

"You crazy," he repeated. "And you don't know what fire is."

"Move over, Cassandra. You're not driving home."

"Fine."

Woody had not yet asked what I knew he was dying to ask: Was it true? Had I really slept with Melvin? There were so many other things to sort out, worry about first. And deep down, he really didn't want to hear my answer, because he knew I never lied to him.

We'd gone back to the university and waited until nine o'clock near the room where Tonia Riddle's eight o'clock class met. She never showed.

He took the Lake Shore Drive to our place.

"I'll wait until you're inside," he said.

"What do you mean? Aren't you coming in?"

"No. I'm going to look in on Ivy. I may not get back tonight."

"I'll come, too."

"No, you won't. You go upstairs. Don't you have home-work or something?"

"Woody, I haven't been to classes since God knows when. I have no idea what the assignments are."

"That's no way for you to be acting."

"Besides that, the rumor is, SDS is going to shut the campus down if the regents fire Bluestein. There won't be any classes to go to."

"Get up there and read something anyway."

"Like what?"

"How the hell do I know? Just find something and read it, goddammit."

EIGHTEEN

That next night was a cool night, and a rare night. Not too often you see stars in the city sky.

Waiting for Tonia Riddle to appear. Again. When she did, she was in a terrible hurry. She flew out of the Ellis Street apartment building and went directly to the modest dark-colored Volkswagen Woody and I had been watching for more than two hours. Jack Klaus had confirmed the license plate for us.

Tonia drove and drove, steadily north. She stopped at a location I rarely had occasion to visit—the Cabrini-Green projects, off North Avenue. As though life at Cabrini-Green weren't ugly enough already, it was squarely in the middle of some of the worst damage from the uprising after King's assassination. The South Side fires were nothing compared to this. I was so caught up in looking at the devastation, I nearly missed the figure that raced like a frantic mouse out of the doorway of a shattered household supplies store, then climbed into the passenger seat of the VW.

Tonia lit out of there. She had never even cut the engine.

Woody checked the glove compartment, opening and closing it softly, as though he didn't dare make a noise.

"What's in there?" I asked.

"Good driving, Cass," he said. "Just keep your eye on the sparrow."

I didn't repeat my question. I could pretty much guess what he had been looking at in the glove compartment. It wasn't a ham sandwich.

My skin, my bloodstream was alive, like a million tiny pin pricks. Kind of a goody-goody with drugs, I'd only smoked a little grass and taken a few amphetamines in order to cram for tests. I didn't know firsthand how LSD made you feel. Must be something like this. What was the usual rhapsodic line about taking acid—you become so *aware* of everything around you, they said.

I was aware, all right. I knew we were heading into some kind of storm. My being knew it.

I got a little worried when Tonia headed for the bright

lights of North Clark Street, one of the main arteries on this side of town. It would be all too easy to lose her in traffic. But she turned off again, onto an empty lot near Dickens. I had to stay at the far end of the block for fear she and her passenger would notice us.

No movement in the Volkswagen. They were obviously keeping as low a profile as we were.

We waited, eyes on the VW, not talking. Finally Woody looked at his watch. "This is taking longer than I figured, Cass. I'm supposed to check in with Jack, give him our location."

"What should we do?"

"There's a coffee shop on the next corner. I'll use the phone there."

"What do you mean! Get out of the car?"

"I have to. You keep yourself together until I get back. And if there's any sign they've seen you, you drive out of here as fast as you can. No questions asked. Go straight home. Understand?"

"Yes. You watch it, too."

He opened the passenger door ever so slightly, slipped out and was gone. The darkness took him.

I slid down a bit further, took my glasses off and gave them a quick cleaning with the tail of my shirt. It reminded me of a conversation I'd once had with Owen. I was ugly, misshapen, red haired, and walked with a slight limp, I told him. Only one thing was missing: spectacles. And at about age thirteen I got them, too.

Woody was back in less than fifteen minutes.

"Anything?"

"No," I said.

"Well, at least we got the proof now. Somebody from the group that nigger Melvin is in with has something to do with Lavelle Jackson. I bet they know who gunned Ivy."

His voice was a near whisper. It just made what he was saying sound all the more vile and frightening.

"How do you know all that?"

"Jack says the weapon that Lavelle was hiding came from the robbery of a gun shop up on the far North Side. Place has been hit more than once. Cops surprised the niggers in the act the last time. Killed one of 'em. The other one got away. The dead one was part of some nigger nonsense called Root, and your boyfriend Melvin is in it right up to his ears."

"Shut up!"

Those words came out of my throat all on their own. I hadn't meant to speak to him that way. I understood why he was looking at me as if I were insane.

"I'm sorry. I'm sorry. But how do you think the police know who's in that group? They spy on people, Woody. They harass, they tap phones. Oh look, it's just—I'm sick of hearing you call them niggers in that awful, nasty way. Did it ever occur to you not everybody lives the way you do, thinks the way you do? What do you know about them, Woody? Some people are trying to build a revolution in this fucking country."

"*Revolution?* Girl, are you out of your mind? Is that what you thought you were doing by laying with that crude nigger—starting a revolution? Don't you turn your face away from me, Cass. They almost killed Ivy. She's the closest thing to a mother you have and you're taking their part?"

"I'm not taking their part. I'm—"

"Hush, girl!"

The headlights of a light-colored two-door blinked on and off as it swung into the lot where Tonia and her companion waited. I could see the driver. A white man. No other passengers. The VW blinked, too, as if it was flirting with the bigger car.

Whitey got out and closed his door noisily.

Aping his movements, Tonia stepped out of the VW.

Their next moves had a weird kind of synchronicity, too. She bent her knees slightly and assumed a firing stance. So did the white driver.

And at the same moment that Tonia's passenger burst out of the VW, his counterpart, who had been hiding, rolled out of the passenger side of the light car.

Then the guns began to splutter.

We watched in horror while the four figures circled and ducked, ran, fired, yelped. And then I proceeded to do the one thing no sane person would. I put my foot on the gas and drove straight toward the mayhem.

Why? Because by then I had recognized Tonia's mystery passenger. It was Bobby.

At the entrance to the lot, Woody was screaming and snatching at me, trying to hold me back. But I fought him off and ran.

The guns had stopped.

Midway between the two automobiles, Tonia lay face up on the gravel, a hole where one of her pale eyes used to be; the other one was staring dreamily at the moon.

Bobby grabbed me and pulled me down near the back wheel of the VW. He held me by the shoulders, looking at me, feeling the weight of my body as though he were trying to make sure I wasn't a ghost.

I saw Woody bend over one of the downed men, inspect him briefly, and then spit. Then he walked briskly over to the VW. He was aiming the long snout of his pistol at Bobby's head.

"Don't!" I screamed.

I sprang up like a snake and began to fight him. Then Bobby got into it. Together we twisted the gun away from Woody, who looked at me in disbelieving rage as he cursed us.

"Get out of here," I screamed at Bobby. "Go."

In the dented little Beetle, he fumbled at the dashboard for a few seconds, and then zoomed out of the lot.

The second man on the ground, the driver, moaned a little. Still alive.

Woody grabbed his pistol from my hand and went to him, ripped at his bloody shirt and revealed an obscene sucking wound.

The man mumbled something and Woody knelt next to him. "You better save it, mister," Woody said. "You got some serious damage there."

"No no no. Now or never."

"Go 'head then."

I swear, the bloody man laughed. I can also testify that the next thing he said was, "You monkeys. You goddamn monkeys."

Woody pulled away from him. "Who?" he shouted. "Poor ass cracker, what are you talking about?"

The guy cackled again, drooling blood. "Waddell—dumb motherfucker—monkey. Tell him I said that. Tell him I been skimming—fucking him—all the while—"

"Did he say Waddell?" I asked.

Woody shushed me. "Go ahead," he told the man, who was gasping like an asthmatic now.

"... you—you revolution monkeys—smarter than him, huh? Lot smarter."

"Yeah, that's right," Woody said, prompting the man,

who had gone quiet. But Woody persisted. "Isn't that right, mister?"

There were only a few seconds more of breath in the guy. He used them to say, "Fuck that other moke, too. Shoulda offed him long ago. His junk store—his little nigger piece on the side. Glad they torched it—glad. Too bad he wasn't inside."

"Who's that you shoulda killed? You mean Carl Garrick? With the hardware store? Look here, you cracker. What about a woman who was shot on Forest Street? What do you know about it?"

No more invective, no more evil laughter, even though Woody had him by the neck then, shaking him.

I touched his shoulder. "He's dead, Woody."

Jack Klaus's Chevy swung onto the lot then. He jumped out from behind the wheel and took in the carnage. "Jesus," he muttered. "You do any of this, Woody?"

"No."

"Good thing."

"This one," Woody said. "It's Zeke Shelton, isn't it?"

"Damn right," said Klaus. He reached into Shelton's jacket and withdrew his shield and wallet. "Who's the other one?"

He meant the black man lying dead near Shelton's car.

"Looks like the one who killed my nephew," Woody said.

I looked again at the still figure, legs splayed. Woody was right. It was him.

We heard the sirens then.

"Good time for you and Cass to blow. This'll be an all-night thing. Lay low until I call you."

I got behind the wheel of Ivy's Buick, turned the key, pulled out. Don't look back. Good advice. I didn't.

Woody was dazed, furious, depleted—all at the same time.

We'd be having an all-night thing, too. I was sure of it.

NINETEEN

Even bred in the bone, city people sometimes want to touch nature, picnic in the woods, camp out in a facsimile of the real wilderness. There are forest preserves no more than a couple of hours' drive from the Loop where folks can do this. I have never set foot in one, and I never will. To me, the forest preserves don't mean summer picnics and Scouting jamborees. I've heard one news bulletin too many for that. They mean biker gangs and gang rapes, the hacked-up bodies of young girls, and Mafia snitches with well-placed shots to the back of the head.

I often thought, during that unprecedented April, that Lavelle Jackson was probably lying in some mossy stretch in a forest preserve. I figured her grandfather would not live long enough to learn where she had been dumped, let alone see her killer brought to justice. I figured he kind of knew that all along. Worse things had happened to people on Forest Street—and been forgotten.

Zeke Shelton's murder, by contrast, was front-page news. It tied in beautifully with the many stories the papers had been running about the Black Nationalist peril. Authorities determined that the dead girl at the scene, Tonia Riddle, had been part of such a group, but they had yet to identify her cohort, who had escaped.

The black man who died at Zeke Shelton's side was variously described as a police informant, a bystander, and a former delinquent whom Shelton was grooming for a career with the department. That was all crap, start to finish. Jack Klaus told us that Uncle Hero's killer was one James Alton. He had been a stooge for Henry Waddell, doubling as hired muscle for Zeke Shelton.

Funny, in a perfect example of injustice for all, Henry Waddell was the only one to come out of the murders, the scandals, the loss and grief, without a scratch. He'd go on conducting his nasty business with the help of some other rotten cop. Not a fucking thing would happen to him.

Whatever investigating there was to be done, Jack Klaus was supervising it. He and Woody spoke every day. Klaus's stock in the department had gone way up since he brought in the Tonia Riddle trophy and was able to help police brass construct a believable tissue of lies to hand the public. Zeke Shelton had brought enough dishonor on the cops during his long career. And since he'd no doubt taken a lot of dirty secrets to his grave, the higher-ups were relieved to have him six feet under.

Ivy's body was on the mend but her spirits were low. All the time, low. She pestered Woody until he admitted what had happened to Hero, and that naturally led, one ugly detail at a time, to his revealing the whole story.

She was propped up in her hospital bed when we arrived one morning. She wore one of her gorgeous beaded bed jackets but looked lost in it somehow, shrunken. "So where is this Garrick?" she asked as soon as we walked in. "Are they looking for him?"

"He's gone," Woody said. "He could be anywhere by now. But Garrick can't be hooked to any of this mess. Not so far, anyway. The police don't have anything to charge him with."

"What about the Jackson girl?"

Woody shook his head.

"Has her grandfather lost hope? Have you, Woody?"

"Jack says the cops have her listed as presumed dead."

She wiped brutally at her tears and her expression turned to disgust. "Can't kill us fast enough, can they?" she said. "Godalmighty, what's the use?"

I took her hand and kissed it but I don't think she even noticed.

"Baby, you should stop working yourself up and rest," Woody told her. "Don't, you'll never get well."

She ignored him. "Didn't Jack Klaus ever get anything out of that hard little whore June? What was she doing at the Riddle girl's apartment on Ellis? What was she doing, mixed up in that political party that Tonia Riddle was in? June didn't go to college like these other people. She only knows how to sell sex and make babies."

Woody was trying to calm her. "We don't know just how she was mixed up with 'em, Ivy. June is a tough one. She told Jack a story he had to accept because he couldn't break her no further. She claims she didn't know what the Riddle girl was into, and didn't want to know.

"Turns out June had known the Riddle girl for years. Her mother used to clean for Tonia Riddle's family. All she admits to is stashing packages the Riddle girl would ask her to hold from time to time. Sometimes Tonia came and picked up the packages and sometimes a man would come. June says Tonia Riddle was paying her to keep her baby, raise the little girl along with her own kid."

Tonia's little girl. Lord. Of course. The children in the playpen at June's place were about the same age. They couldn't have both been June's. I couldn't help wondering if the baby had been fathered by one of the men in Root.

Melvin? Maybe even Bobby. I also had to wonder where that little girl would be in ten years, no mother, no father. Sadness punched at my heart.

Ivy's voice was like gravel. "I hope they at least break up that goddamn whorehouse. Four hundred years and we can't think of anything better to do than sell each other. It's all such horrible shit."

I'd rarely heard Ivy talk like that. Woody was so upset by it, he went off to find the doctor, to beg him to give her something to settle her down. She needn't have worried about the whorehouse, though. It was pretty much broken up. With all the attention June was getting from the police, the customers were taking their needs elsewhere.

On the way home, Woody at the wheel, I thought about some of the news Ivy didn't know about at all, like the heat that had been turned all the way up at school. As on so many other campuses, students protesting the war and the dismissal of a radical professor had occupied the dean's office and in effect closed down the college.

The Root office was empty now, not so much as a rubber band left behind. I had no idea where Melvin was. But since rumors were circulating about illegal taps on the office phone, maybe the police knew more about him than I did.

There were all sorts of wars going on. The one between Woody and me wasn't anything you could read about in the newspaper. It had its firefights, its truces, and standoffs. But it was private. We worked hard to keep Ivy in the dark about it. I was as immovable as June Barker; I never gave him the name of Tonia's companion and I steadfastly refused to discuss my relationship with Melvin.

He started to grill me about Melvin—again—when we were halfway home, and a half an hour later, in the apartment, he was still at it. I knew we were headed for another explosive argument. Who knows how it might have ended if the phone hadn't rung when it did. Who knows what awful things we might have said to each other if it hadn't been for Lucille Crooks, also known as Blubber Butt.

The grounds of Champlain Elementary were all but deserted. The students and the teachers had all gone home. But not Lucille Crooks, who was waiting at the front entrance to escort us to her office.

"I've received a letter," she announced. "It was sent to me, but your name is on it as well."

Woody waited for her to go on.

"Mr. Lisle, I'm well aware of the position you hold in this community. But as I told you before, I will not have this school disrupted."

"It's good to know you're looking out for the children," he answered.

"I give this to you in the hope you'll exercise discretion."

I saw the postmark on the handwritten envelope: Flagstaff, Arizona.

Woody pulled out two sheets of ordinary lined notebook paper. But before he read the words written on them, he looked for a signature at the end of the letter. There was none.

He went back and read the first page carefully, then handed it to me while he read page two.

"Tom Springer is a bad and dangerous man," the first line read.

But he is my half brother. He has a record for hurting women and girls back home where we are from in Fort Wayne. Except he was known there under the name Tom Garrick. I thought and worried that maybe some children might have been hurt while he was at the school, probably they were. He swore he wasn't doing anything bad. But I never knew for sure. You couldn't trust him even when he was a child.

Years ago he raped and killed a teacher at the Champlain School. I think she may have known his secret. I think she maybe caught him doing something with one of those kids. With my help and another man, the cop named Zeke Shelton, Tom didn't go to jail. Instead we let a Negro boy go. Tom swore it wasn't him who did anything sexual to that teacher, even though he admitted he killed her. He says that boy was the one responsible for that, a kid not right in the head who raped her after she was dead. Is it true? Nobody will ever know.

Why did Zeke agree to get Tom out of trouble for me? I knew many things he has done. That's why. He has a background of being in with drug dealers. Lots of people already know about that. But they don't know he killed a man who was in the way of Waddell, his boss who paid for Zeke's boat and new cars and the property he has here and other places.

How do I know about this murder being done? Because I personally saw him do it. How and where did he do the killing? I won't say for fear of the police coming for me some day too. But I know.

I have no right to complain about him because I knew what he was like but I went on taking favors from him. I had something on him, that's for sure. But he had some things on me too. That's how we got along. (Like I said, I am not telling the things I did.)

There was a girl named Lavelle. A fast girl and I should have never gone with her. But no matter what you say about her, she was a lot better than people knew. Yes she was a prostitute. But smart. I always told her she was too smart for her own good. She had a mind of her own just the same. I might as well admit I loved her, prostitute or no.

I did not know she was going with my brother Tom once in a while. I found out about that when it was too late. That was the thing about Lavelle, nobody could make her do anything. She said she wasn't ever going to answer to anybody. Anyway, she found out about Tom and about Zeke too, and I found out later that she told *another man, a Negro I saw with her and got jealous about. Yes I was jealous and I asked her next time I saw her who he was. She said he was only some cousin of her friend June's. I asked if he was a pimp or something. She denied it, but I didn't believe her. I said "I saw him with his hands on you." She laughed and said "So what? I will put my hands on you and you won't worry no more, nothing else will matter." She was right. It didn't matter. I loved her and I wanted her and couldn't help myself. But she wanted me too. Maybe you think that's a lie but a man knows when a girl is lying about that.*

Anyway I guess Lavelle and this colored guy thought they could put the pressure on Zeke and I guess for a little while they did. But not forever. You can't trust Zeke Shelton any farther than you can throw him. When I heard Lavelle was gone missing, I knew who had done it. And I knew she must be dead.

I hate Zeke for what he did to Lavelle and I hate my half brother too. But I also have hated myself for a long long time and can't live with all of it inside me anymore. Also, I knew enough to know Zeke would probably come after me next. He knew good and well what I felt about Lavelle and he probably figured I'd be so mad I might tell everything. He is dead now and I'm glad for that, which means it can all come out and maybe help that kid that went to jail. I don't know.

My family life is over. I'll never go back to Chicago and who knows, maybe won't ever see my kid again. I guess he will hate me forever too. Now I don't have Lavelle any longer either. It hurts me

to know she was murdered like it hurts me to know I will never be
with her in bed again. She didn't believe in God and neither did I.
But I think probably we will all be punished for the things we did.

"Is he still in the building?" Woody asked the principal.

"I believe so. I told him the superintendent was visiting tomorrow and we needed some repairs done in the auditorium. I said they had to be finished by morning."

"Did he seem suspicious about that?"

"No. He was happy to hear it. He makes double-time wages for work done after school hours. In addition to being bone stupid, he is also greedy."

Lucille Crooks lifted both eyebrows then. I could imagine her wearing a monocle. *Grrree-day,* she pronounced it, rolling the hell out of that *r* and reminding me so much of the buxom, prissy woman in those Marx Brothers' movies. Owen loves it when Groucho scandalizes her.

"What do you intend to do, Mr. Lisle?" Mrs. Crooks asked.

"I won't hurt him unless he makes me."

"Discretion," she said loudly. "I want your word. After all, I didn't have to show you the letter."

"I know," said Woody.

I knew the way to the auditorium.

The stars and stripes looked tired and dirty hanging up

there above the wooden stage. *Our flag was still there.* Another blow of memory like a rolling pin to the head. Standing at attention and singing the anthem every Wednesday. Spitballs landing on the back of my neck. We freaks—bookworms, ugly kids, stutterers, tattletales—fearing most of all those times when they made us watch a film, because then we were in the dark and God only knew what was going to happen to us.

Springer was banging nails into the bottom of a wooden chair. There was an open can of spackle near his hand, screwdrivers, glue, oil can, workmen's gloves scattered around him.

He looked up when we walked in, apparently untroubled by our appearance. Blubber Butt might think he was entirely stupid, but I knew better. I figured he was sharp enough, in any case, to know we could do him no real harm. Zeke Shelton was dead. His half brother, Garrick, was on the run, not likely to come back to Chicago just to accuse him. Lavelle was out of the picture. All he had to do was stick to his old story. Even if he wound up losing his job because of past crimes, he'd still be a free man.

Woody caught me by the arm. "Stand back," he said. "Just sit till I tell you to move."

I perched on the arm of a chair and watched him walk the rest of the way down the center aisle.

"What say, old Rastus?" Tom Springer asked.

"Forgot my name, did you?" Woody kicked out suddenly, and Springer was on his back. A second later blood was flying out of his mouth along with a front tooth.

The younger man recovered quickly. Back on his feet, he lunged for Woody. But the butt of Woody's gun against his temple broke up that move.

"How's that feel?" Woody shouted. "You let that boy take the beating you were owed. How do you like it, cracker?"

Springer was reeling. With little effort, Woody shoved him into the nearest seat. "You killed that teacher. Ripped her apart. If you say you didn't I'll shoot you right now."

Springer mewled. I began inching my way closer to them.

"You know what happened to Lavelle Jackson, too. Isn't that right?"

Frantic denials until Woody whomped him across the face.

"Did you hear me, you murdering idiot? You help Shelton kill her? Where'd y'all hide her body?"

I don't know if Tom Springer genuinely believed Woody was going to shoot him. He must have. Because he called on whatever cunning he had left to attempt a lethal thrust then. Just as the blade of Woody's razor had sparkled that day in the bar with Luther, the hammer that was suddenly in Tom Springer's fist caught the light from the overhead fixture. He was bringing it downward, onto Woody's head. My scream came just in time. Woody fell heavily to the side, escaping the blow.

Enough time for Springer to try a bust out. He ran for the exit, moving like a tiny bush animal.

By the time Woody was up again, Springer had a good twenty seconds on us. The side door hung open and I could see him booking across the parking lot, glancing back over his left shoulder as he ran.

I also saw the blue Cadillac backing out of the principal's parking spot. And I heard the hideous thunk it made as it punched into Tom Springer's torso. He went soaring into the air and landed across the way like a bag of dirty clothes.

EPILOGUE

Classes resumed just in time for the semester to end. The occupation of the dean's office had terminated in the predictable way—Mayor Daley's cops waded in, cracked some heads, and several dozen students spent the night in lockup. But by then, that sort of thing was an everyday occurrence. *Same song, second verse,* to borrow a phrase Ivy used a lot.

The merry month of May. My God, the weather was lovely. The parks were flowering in heartbreaking pinks and yellows. Young people were everywhere you looked, as if our population was doubling every night while the rest of the world slept. And although it often seemed our elders wanted us dead for being young, the heady, arrogant sense that we owned all beauty and right spread among us like a druggy virus. Dope smoking, acid dropping, random fucking, and generalized defiance were at an all-time high.

Yes, I was one of the young. However, I took little joy in that. I didn't feel young anymore. Before we could approach Eddie Lee Quick's attorney with the information we had uncovered, we learned that the boy had recently been beaten to death in the prison laundry.

Closer to home, my Aunt Ivy looked like something that had been left in the water too long; she was eating through a tube. Half the time, Woody wasn't even speaking to me. And Bobby. Bobby never came back.

Thus, on the average day there was not much laughter in my life.

We'd had a campus tragedy, too—well, if Daniel Bluestein's dismissal did not rise to the level of tragedy, certainly it was a defeat, the loss of a gifted teacher who was on our side.

Some thought that RFK's certain election would pull us out of Vietnam and turn back the wave of poverty and hopelessness in the cities. But in the meantime, violence on our South Side skyrocketed and life in the little town of Forest Street did not change.

Nothing could stop the beautification of the Loop, though. It went forward at a brisk pace. Chicago was going to host the Democratic National Convention that summer.

Would it be a carnival or a bloodbath? The downtown merchants were licking their chops. And the serious politicos in Owen's SDS-saturated part of town were wearing a button that said FLOWER POWER, THAT WAS *LAST* SUMMER.

I was volunteering two days a week at a preschool/free school in the same area where I'd last seen Bobby. Most of the kids were from the Cabrini-Green projects. The man who started the school was an old-line Negro Socialist. Once or twice I'd gone to a folk music concert with him and wound up spending the night at his sad little apartment on Vine Street. And if we could not provide the children with paramilitary training and Huey Newton berets, we were at least supplying them with whole milk, crayons they could keep, and stories about Harriet Tubman.

On the last day of the term at Debs, I was eating an Almond Joy while I pulled old papers out of my locker, down the hall from Owen's office. He and I were planning to have drinks when I was through. I looked up and saw him moving toward me, fast. Owen was nice and willowy, and from all appearances in perfect health, but I don't know that I'd ever seen him running anywhere for anything before that day.

"Come into my office," he said. "Put that stuff down."

"What's happening?"

He leaned in. "Hurry. Bobby Vaughan's on the phone."

* * *

That afternoon I told Woody the first of many half truths and straight-up lies. I needed the car, I said, to go to a lecture at Northwestern, the university in nearby Evanston. And I wanted to offer my professor a lift out there as well.

I picked Owen up at his place and then swung onto the Eisenhower Expressway. The suburbs get posher as you continue north. Bobby was waiting at a donut shop in Skokie, a settled, predominantly Jewish area with pockets of white and black working-class people. During that brief phone conversation, there had been no time to ask him how the hell he'd wound up in Skokie. I just took down the address and said I'd follow his instructions.

A dancing neon donut, twenty feet high, let us know we'd found the place. Owen waited in the parking lot while I went in.

I saw Bobby at once. He was in overalls, pushing a broom.

I didn't even dare say his name. I just ordered coffee and a glazed donut and took it to the molded plastic table in the rear. He came over a minute later and sat across from me. We didn't touch.

"Is it okay to talk?" I asked. And I pushed a copy of *Ramparts* over to his side of the table. There were three hundred-dollar bills clipped in there, my savings, and another hundred and fifty that Owen gave me.

"Thanks, Cassandra."

"Not necessary. Just tell me, like you said you would. I mean, tell me as much as you can."

"Okay. Man who was at the head of our thing, Root, his name was Wilson. The last few months he had been setting up these beautiful scores for us. Guns and other stuff that could get us quick cash. We were bopping into these stores and warehouses with no trouble. It was so easy, we knew Wilson had to have an in somewhere. I mean, how else could he know when deliveries were coming in, when security guards changed their shifts, stuff like that. We started to think Wilson must know some brother who had infiltrated the pigs and was acting like a double agent or something. Wilson wouldn't tell us who was tipping him. But we figured, whoever it was, they must be on our side.

"Come to find out, that wasn't it. Not exactly. This brother in Root, his name was Hoyt, he found out Wilson was blackmailing a pig detective name-a Zeke Shelton who was fat from South Side heroin money. This Shelton was in with Henry Waddell. He's a filthy rich black bastard who—"

"I know who he is. Go ahead."

"Okay. So Wilson had something on this pig Shelton. Not the heroin thing. Something else. Hoyt kept his eyes and ears open and picked up some of the story. Shelton had railroaded some young brother into jail a few years back. He put the kid away for raping and killing some white woman.

Wasn't nothing new about that. The thing was, Shelton knew exactly who really did it. You dig what I'm saying? He didn't just plant evidence and shit. He actually covered for the murderer."

"And how did Wilson know all this?" I asked.

" 'Cause of a girl he was going with. A fast young thing who hooks. She told him the story. One of her tricks was this redneck clown who can't hold his liquor. One night the girl is in his crib, see. She goes snooping around while he's passed out. Finds something in the apartment and steals it. Few days later he realizes it's gone and he goes crazy.

"He calls her one day, says he got plenty of money and wants to get it on with her again. But when she shows up, he comes after her strong. He wanted what she took from him, see. But the girl surprised him. She pulled a gun on him. By the time it was over, he had pretty much straight out confessed to killing that white woman, *and* he tells her about Shelton, the pig who hushed it up. Whatever it was this whore took, it ties this honky to the crime."

So, at last "Afro" had a real name: Wilson. He was the Negro that Carl Garrick had spotted with Lavelle. But he was no pimp. He was the main man behind Root. He was also the man who sometimes picked up those packages that Tonia Riddle was hiding at june Barker's place. On one of his visits there, he must've met Lavelle Jackson and fallen under her spell.

"I don't suppose you know who the girl was. The hooker, I mean."

"No. I don't know who the redneck motherfucker is either."

I made the decision then. I wouldn't give Bobby the honky trick's name: Tom Springer. Nor would I tell him the rest of the Lavelle Jackson/Eddie Quick story. We had little enough time, and there wasn't a damn thing he could do, anyway.

"Go ahead," I said. "The Root guy—Wilson—is squeezing the crooked cop. The crooked cop is setting up robberies for you guys so you'll have guns and ammunition and ready cash for when the apocalypse hits, right?"

"Right."

"And then, on this one particular robbery, the gun shop on Sheridan Road, something goes wrong."

"That doesn't even half say it. The two Root men who were taking off the gun shop were ambushed. The cops were waiting for them when they walked in. One of them was lucky. He got away. The other one was blown to pieces."

"Was that your friend Hoyt?"

"Yes."

"And the one who got away was Wilson?"

"Naw. That's just it. Wilson was down to do the job with Hoyt. But he pulled out at the last minute. Said he had a meeting with some cats in Michigan. He sent somebody else to do the robbery with Hoyt."

"Somebody named Melvin. Correct?"

I couldn't tell from Bobby's look how much he knew about Melvin and me, but he wasn't surprised that I knew the name. "I don't want to get into that," he said. "The main thing is, it was a setup. And Wilson must've known from the git there was gonna be a setup. He knew Shelton was out to kill him. Shelton expected Wilson to open that gun shop door and walk into a bullet. Guess he figured 'Fuck whoever had the bad luck to be with Wilson that night.' "

"No doubt."

"I bet he thought he'd get rid of Wilson first and then go after the hooker who had this evidence."

"Good guess. But Wilson didn't get killed that night. So what happened to him?"

Bobby looked down at the magazine cover.

"What?"

"He cleaned us out and he split. Guns, money, he took it all. We found out he was selling weapons to any mother-fucker, black or white, who could meet his price. You get it? He was pushing those guns to niggers who were going to turn right around and use them against our people. In-nocent black people looking to us to end this goddamn system, stop the exploitation. He must've been laughing his ass off at us. He thought he and that little whore would be living high on the hog somewhere."

"But . . . ?"

Bobby's mouth twisted then. Not exactly a smile, you couldn't call it that. "Let's just say we found him. And his laughing days are over."

I looked around before speaking, and when I did, I whispered, "You mean you killed—executed him?"

"Purged."

"Did you—did Melvin—"

"What difference does it make who? The will of the group was carried out. He's gone, Cassandra. An enemy of the people is gone. That's all you need to know."

"You never found the girl, though."

He shook his head.

"And Melvin? Is he safe?"

"I can't talk about Bounia."

"*Who?*"

"Bounia. Melvin took an African name."

"Oh." Right. Maybe someday I'd get to sleep with another man. Maybe he'd surprise and teach and elate me as Melvin had done. Maybe he'd be using the name his mother gave him. Maybe Uncle Woody wouldn't take one look at him and want to saw him in half. Maybe. But I had learned not to count on such things.

"Meanwhile," I said, "you and Tonia. That night."

"Tonia and me drew the assignment to hit Shelton. Not just for getting Hoyt killed but for all the shit he had done in his worthless life. We tracked him down, called him and handed him a bullshit story. Told him we had the evidence he was looking for, said we were gonna sell it to him. I don't even know if he really swallowed that. I think he knew what was going to go down and decided to strike first. We'll never know the answer to that. But you know what happened. You saw Tonia buy it. You saw Shelton get it, too. And whoever that was in the car with him. A black undercover pig, I guess."

"No, not that. He was a thug who'd been in Shelton's pocket for a long time. He did a lot of dirty work for him, including murder."

He stood then, rolled the magazine up, and commenced to clear off my table.

"Are you taking care of yourself?" I asked.

He smiled a little then. "I'm all right."

"What are you doing here, anyway? Is this some kind of safe house?"

"No. I got a job here. Good cover. I been living with some people a few miles out. But now I'm set to go. When I leave for work tomorrow, they'll never see me again."

Never. I hated the sound of that word. I remembered something then, an occasion when I'd said that one word to Bobby. He took me to a party once. Not as his date, of course. And it wasn't a Root thing either, just some people he knew getting together for fun. He got high, and when somebody found a 45 of "Pride and Joy," he began to pull me into the center of the room, trying to make me dance with him.

I went into a panic. "I can't," I kept telling him.

"Don't tell me you never dance," he said.

"Never," I said.

"Well, you gone dance now."

I had been in Bobby's arms a thousand times in my imagination. Now it was real. He rocked effortlessly from his pelvis and moved his feet as if he were skating. Before I knew it, I was moving with him, deep down in the beat. Man, I was lifted out of my shoes, free.

He was looking anxiously at me now. "Cassandra?"

"What did you say?"

"Everything okay?"

How was I supposed to answer that?

He said, "I better go."

"Just one more thing. I just want to know—do you think *I'll* ever see you again?"

He nodded. I tried my best to believe him.

Then came the hardest part: I had to get myself up and out of my seat without calling his name, without touching him, without following him with my eyes. *Don't look back.* I didn't.

Outside again, I handed the car keys to Owen, who took them without a word.